How to . . .

get the most from your
COLES NOTES

Key Point

Basic concepts in point form.

Close Up

Additional hints, notes, tips or background information.

Watch Out!

Areas where problems frequently occur.

Quick Tip

Concise ideas to help you learn what you need to know.

Remember This!

Essential material for mastery of the topic.

Margaret Atwood's

The Handmaid's Tale

—————— ABOUT COLES NOTES ——————

COLES NOTES have been an indispensable aid to students on five continents since 1948.

COLES NOTES now offer titles on a wide range of general interest topics as well as traditional academic subject areas and individual literary works. All COLES NOTES are written by experts in their fields and reviewed for accuracy by independent authorities and the Coles Editorial Board.

COLES NOTES provide clear, concise explanations of their subject areas. Proper use of COLES NOTES will result in a broader understanding of the topic being studied. For academic subjects, COLES NOTES are an invaluable aid for study, review and exam preparation. For literary works, COLES NOTES provide interesting interpretations and evaluations which supplement the text but are not intended as a substitute for reading the text itself. Use of the NOTES will serve not only to clarify the material being studied, but should enhance the reader's enjoyment of the topic.

© Copyright 2002 and Published by
COLES PUBLISHING. A division of Prospero Books
Toronto – Canada
Printed in Canada

National Library of Canada Cataloguing in Publication

Brandon, Paul, 1947-
Margaret Atwood's The handmaid's tale.

(Coles notes)
Written by Paul Brandon and R.S. Dinsmore.
Includes index.
ISBN 0-7740-3870-5

1. Atwood, Margaret, 1939- Handmaid's tale.
I. Dinsmore, Robert S., 1940- II. Title. III. Series.

PS8501 T86 H353 2002   C813'.54   C2002-902760-8
PR9199.3.A8H33 2002

Editing: Paul Kropp Communications
Book design : Karen Petherick, Markham, Ontario
Layout : Chris Belfontaine

Manufactured by Webcom Limited
Cover finish: Webcom's Exclusive DURACOAT

Contents

Chapter One

Margaret Atwood: Life and works

Margaret Atwood was born in Ottawa, in 1939. She grew up in Ottawa, Sault Ste. Marie and Toronto. When she was about sixteen years old, Atwood decided that she wanted to be a writer. She wrote poems and stories for the Leaside High School magazine, as well as a humorous "home economics" opera about synthetic fabrics — Old King Coal and three princesses Nylon, Dacron and Orlon.

During four years at Victoria College, University of Toronto, she continued to write. By the end of her honors B.A. program, Atwood had published her first poetry collection, *Double Persephone* (1961). She won a prestigious Woodrow Wilson scholarship for post-graduate work at Radcliffe College, what was then the women's college of Harvard University. She completed a master's degree in Victorian literature in 1962 and began Ph.D. studies, which she did not finish. Instead, she left Harvard to teach at several Canadian schools, including the University of British Columbia and Sir George Williams University in Montreal. She wrote her first novel, *The Edible Woman*, in 1965 while at U.B.C.

In the early 1970s, Atwood travelled in England, France and Italy, and in 1972 returned to the University of Toronto as writer-in-residence. From the 1970s onward, she established herself as an important voice in Canadian letters. Her published works include important nonfiction titles, such as *Survival: A Thematic Guide to Canadian Literature* (1972), several poetry and story collections, as well as novels. Atwood has been recognized internationally and awarded numerous prizes for her work. Since 1980, she has lived in Toronto with novelist Graeme Gibson. They have one daughter, Jess, now in her twenties.

Atwood has used her fame and influence in the Canadian literary scene to support several important causes — Canadian literary nationalism, the women's movement, Amnesty International and the Writers' Union of Canada.

Major works

Short fiction collections

Dancing Girls 1977
Murder in the Dark 1983
Bluebeard's Egg 1983
Wilderness Tips 1991
Good Bones 1992

Novels

The Edible Woman 1969
Surfacing 1972
Lady Oracle 1976
Life Before Man 1979
Bodily Harm 1981
The Handmaid's Tale 1985
Cat's Eye 1989
The Robber Bride 1993
Alias Grace 1996
The Blind Assassin 2000

Poetry

For Children

Nonfiction

Chapter Two

Introduction to The Handmaid's Tale

In an interview published in *MS* magazine (February 1986), Margaret Atwood said that she put off writing *The Handmaid's Tale* for four years, because she thought it was too "zany" and "unconventional." Then she began another book that "kept wandering off into the subject matter of this one, and I felt that, all right, this is the book I should be writing." It became a "compelling story" that she had to write.

Several contemporary events in the early 1980s contributed to that compulsion. For example, there was a growing public backlash against the sexual permissiveness of the 1970s and the women's liberation movement. Right-wing religious groups – the self-styled "Moral Majority" – were growing in influence and calling for a return to traditional family values. In the Middle East, governments such as Iran's revolutionary Islamic clerics used religious authority to impose narrow restrictions on all citizens, and especially on the social and political roles of women. Around the world, but especially in heavily industrialized countries of the West, scientists were raising serious questions about environmental pollution and its increasingly toxic effects on all life.

Out of these strands, Atwood wove a story of the near future, a speculative and satirical look at where our world might be heading. In form, the novel pretends to be a diary or memoir, recorded by an intelligent, educated young woman known as "Offred," who tries to escape the enforced slavery imposed by a harsh military-religious totalitarian government. Atwood is working in the genre of dystopian fiction – a "negative utopia" that aspires to being a stable, effective social system, but whose underlying flaws, cruelties and corruption are clearly revealed to the reader. Unlike Aldous Huxley's *Brave New World* (1934) or George Orwell's *Nineteen Eighty-Four* (1949), Atwood's novel leaves much of the political structure vague. We see the effects of the regime's restrictive controls, without understanding – any more than Offred can understand – the reasons and methods behind the controls. A brief addition, the "Historical Notes" at the end of the novel, creates an incident two hundred years in the future, when scholars are able to fill in some of the historical details of Offred's time.

Dystopian fiction is satirical in purpose, and *The Handmaid's Tale* is no exception. By illustrating the effects of feminist and anti-feminist conflicts, of unchecked religious extremism, of unscrupulous, male-dominated political opportunism, and of toxic endangerment to the biosphere, Atwood has written a serious warning about the state of the world.

Chapter Three

List of characters

Alma	a Handmaid in training at the Red Center, who passes on Janine's story of Moira's escape
Aunt Elizabeth	instructor in Gynecological Education at the Red Center; threatened and physically restrained by Moira during her successful escape
Aunt Helena	a fat instructor at the Red Center who formerly ran a Weight Watchers' franchise in Iowa; good at Testifying
* Aunt Lydia	principal instructor and disciplinarian of the Handmaids in training at the Red Center; object of Offred's sarcasm and hatred
Aunt Sara	one of the armed disciplinarians in the Red Center dormitory
* Commander (Fred)	Frederick R. Waterford; Offred's Commander at her latest posting; husband of Serena Joy
Commander (Warren)	Janine's (Ofwarren's) Commander, whose home Offred visits on Janine's Birth Day
Cora	Martha in service at Commander Fred's household; general maid
Doctor	male obstetrician-gynecologist, visited by Offred for required monthly examination; offers to "help" Offred in becoming pregnant

Dolores	a Handmaid in training at the Red Center, who passes on Janine's story of Moira's escape
* Janine	Ofwarren; Handmaid who delivers an Unbaby at her Birth Day ritual and later loses her sanity
Luke	Offred's husband, father of her child; a university instructor; disappears, possibly killed, in their unsuccessful escape attempt
* Moira	Offred's best friend at university; a feminist, lesbian, and born rebel; escapes the Red Center and later turns up as a prostitute at Jezebel's
* Nick	a Guardian, assigned as chauffeur to Commander Fred; probably a double agent, both Eye (secret police) and member of Mayday resistance group
* Offred	Handmaid to Commander Fred; narrator and central character, whose taped diary or memoir, as reconstructed two hundred years later, is the novel *The Handmaid's Tale*
Offred's daughter	unnamed; victim of attempted kidnapping at eleven months old; five years old at time of Offred and Luke's attempted escape; about eight years old during the main story
* Offred's mother	unnamed; passionate feminist who participated in marches and demonstrations of the women's movements in the 1970s and 1980s; single parent who bore Offred at age 37
Ofglen	Offred's shopping companion, in touch with underground resistance movement, the Mayday group

Rita	Martha in service at Commander Fred's household; cook
* **Serena Joy**	Wife of Commander Fred; former singer-evangelist named "Pam" on Growing Souls Gospel Hour, then spokesperson in an anti-feminist movement for return to traditional values of home and family

(*Starred names: See detailed notes in the Character Sketches section)

Characters mentioned in "Historical Notes":

Crescent Moon, Maryann	Professor, Department of Caucasian Anthropology, University of Denay, Nunavit; chair of Twelfth Symposium on Gileadean Studies, June 25, 2195
Judd, B. Frederick	possible candidate in attempts to identify Offred's Commander Fred
Limpkin, Wilfred	Gileadean sociobiologist who kept diary in code with useful information for later historians Pieixoto, James Darcy Professor, and Director of Twentieth and Twenty-first Century Archives, Cambridge University; keynote speaker at Twelfth Symposium on Gileadean Studies, June 25, 2195; reconstructed Offred's tape recorded memoir as *The Handmaid's Tale*
Wade, Knotly	Professor, Cambridge University; co-editor (with Pieixoto) of Offred's memoir *The Handmaid's Tale*

8

Chapter Four

The story in brief

Early in the 1980s, a right-wing military coup overthrows the U.S. government and establishes a Christian fundamentalist state, the Republic of Gilead. Under the ruling authority of Commanders, the totalitarian government defends its borders with military forces known as Angels. On the domestic scene, strict control of the populace is maintained by Guardians and by secret police known as Eyes.

The new government's chief concern is a very low birthrate and the need for repopulation. In Gilead, women of child-bearing age are assigned duties as Handmaids. Each Handmaid is assigned to a Commander's household, in order to bear one or more children who will be raised by the Commander's Wife as her own. During a monthly, ritualistic Ceremony, the Commander's Wife participates symbolically in the Commander and Handmaid's act of sexual intercourse. If a viable pregnancy results and is carried to term, a Birth Day ritual again symbolically involves the Wife, as the Handmaid delivers her child.

The first-person narrator of the story is a Handmaid called Offred. Her name ("of Fred") indicates that she serves in the household of Commander Fred. The Commander's Wife is Serena Joy, who was once a television evangelist. As a public figure, she had denounced the feminist movement of the 1970s and had preached a return to traditional values of home and family.

This is Offred's third posting as a Handmaid, her third – and possibly last – chance to produce a child. If she fails, she may be assigned as an Unwoman to the Colonies. This is where older women, failed Handmaids, Gender Traitors (homosexuals) and others are forced to spend their remaining years cleaning up toxic waste sites and disposing of military casualties.

In her story, Offred recalls in flashbacks her life before this posting. As a child, she was sometimes involved against her will in her single mother's feminist campaigns. As a young woman at Harvard University, she enjoyed a free and happy student life with her best friend, Moira. She began an affair with a married instructor named Luke and, after his divorce, married him. They established a home together, but life changed drastically when the coup occurred that created the Republic of Gilead.

The situation under the new military regime grew oppressive. Offred – like most other young women – was forced to quit her job and become totally dependent on her husband. She and Luke, with their infant daughter, tried to escape to Canada using fake passports, but were intercepted. Luke was killed or captured – Offred never knew for sure – and their five-year-old daughter was taken. Offred herself, after a brief traumatic period, was placed in a Re-education Center. There, indoctrination and training of young women capable of bearing children was conducted by the Aunts, dedicated and loyal older women in service to the authorities. Moira was also assigned to the Red Center, and the two met secretly until Moira, always bold and irrepressible, managed to escape.

Three years later, assigned to Commander Fred's household, Offred lives in what was once Cambridge, Massachusetts, close to the former Harvard University. One of her duties is a daily shopping excursion for food, in company with her partner, a Handmaid named Ofglen. They regularly visit the Wall, where executed criminals are hung on public display by the secret police, as warnings to the general populace about duty and obedience.

In the Commander's home, Offred has no formal duties other than keeping herself in physical condition for child-bearing, and playing the central role in the monthly Ceremony with the Commander and Serena Joy. Like all Handmaids, she is required to wear a voluminous red dress and veil, much like a nun's habit, with a covering headdress that has white wings or blinkers to restrict her view of the world, and the world's view of her. In her closet, she discovers a scratched message in crude Latin left by a previous Handmaid. She later learns the meaning: Don't let the bastards grind you down. The other members of the household are a Guardian named Nick, who serves as the Commander's chauffeur (and maybe an Eye), and two Marthas named Rita and Cora, who are domestic servants, cook and maid, respectively.

The main action of the novel covers a period from early spring to late summer. One evening after the monthly Ceremony, Offred is informed by Nick that she is to meet the Commander, secretly, in his private study the following evening.

The next day, Offred participates at the Birth Day ritual of a Handmaid known as Ofwarren. She had been Janine at the Red Center and had been a special pet of Aunt Lydia, one of those in charge. All the Handmaids and Wives of the district are present for the delivery of Janine's baby, which is immediately turned over to the Wife of Commander Warren and named Angela. Later, Offred learns that the child was discovered to be in some way deformed. The infant was declared an Unbaby or shredder, and destroyed.

That evening, Offred goes to the Commander's study, terrified. She hates him for his oppression of her as a Commander, but she finds a more sympathetic and human side to him in private. Commander Fred wants to show her kindness and would like some sincere affection in return. They learn to be more comfortable with each other by playing Scrabble. In subsequent meetings, he shows her his collection of forbidden books and allows her to read women's magazines from the time before the Gilead revolution. Offred begins to enjoy their sessions together. She realizes that in sharing his secret pleasures, she can ask for something in return. At first, she wants something simple: hand lotion for her dry skin. Later she tells him she wants to know more about the world outside her restricted situation.

During a shopping excursion, Ofglen reveals to Offred that she is in touch with an underground resistance group known as Mayday. Offred hopes that Mayday might help her learn the fate of her mother, her husband Luke, her lost daughter and her friend Moira.

When she returns home, Serena Joy speaks to her privately in her garden. She says that Offred's time for becoming pregnant is running out and offers to arrange a secret meeting with Nick, the chauffeur, who may be able to do what the Commander has not. The Wife wants a child to raise. In return for cooperation, she tells Offred she can show her a photograph of her daughter, alive and well.

Some time later, all the women of the district attend a Women's Prayvaganza, a group wedding of Angels, returned from military action on the country's disputed borders, and young daughters of the Commanders' Wives. The same evening, Serena Joy brings Offred's dinner tray and the promised photograph of her child. Offred is grateful but at the same time feels more strongly the anger and hatred for what has been done to her and her family.

At a secret meeting with the Commander that evening, he surprises her with a request to put on makeup and a colorful theatrical costume of feathers and sequins. Then he has Nick drive them to a former hotel, a private club – really a brothel – known as Jezebel's. Officials like himself frequent the place for illicit pleasures not normally available to them in the rigid Gilead society. Commander Fred hopes that this outing will answer questions for Offred and that they will both find some pleasure together in one of the private rooms.

At Jezebel's, Offred meets her old friend Moira, now serving as a prostitute, and learns about her escape from the Red Center and subsequent recapture, torture and assignment at the brothel. Moira provides news also of Offred's mother, now an Unwoman in the Colonies.

At home, later the same night, Serena Joy comes to Offred's room and directs her to the planned secret meeting with Nick. Offred finds reawakened passion in Nick's arms. Despite feeling she is betraying her lost husband Luke, she continues to meet the chauffeur regularly during the summer months.

At another district ceremony, a Women's Salvaging, Offred and the other Handmaids are involved in the public execution of three female criminals. This is followed by a special, horrifying ritual, a Particicution. A male criminal, a Guardian accused of rape, is literally torn apart by enraged Handmaids. Offred does not take an active part, but Ofglen does. When Offred accuses her of brutal behavior, Ofglen reveals that the man had been a political victim, a member of Mayday. She had acted quickly to put him out of his misery.

On the regular shopping trip later the same day, Offred is terrified to find that Ofglen has disappeared, and a new Ofglen has taken her place. Offred fears that her own contacts with the former Ofglen may endanger her, but the new Ofglen tells her that her friend committed suicide when she realized the secret police van was coming for her.

Back home, Offred is stopped by Serena Joy, who has learned about the excursion to Jezebel's. Serena Joy accuses Offred of betrayal, and the Handmaid wonders which of her several crimes – meetings with the Commander, the love affair with Nick, contact with Mayday – will bring her downfall. When a black van approaches the house, it is Nick who comes to her room to lead her out. She is terrified, but he reassures her that the men are members of Mayday and will help her escape. She must trust him as she departs, not knowing whether it will be the end for her, or a new beginning.

Historical notes

About two hundred years after the events Offred has described, an academic conference takes place at the University of Denay, Nunavit. Professor Pieixoto, the main speaker, explains the problems in authenticating the diary or memoir now known as "The Handmaid's Tale." Some time after her escape, Offred managed to record her story on about 30 audio cassettes. Pieixoto has reconstructed this diary and has tried to identify the narrator and others mentioned in it. In doing so, Pieixoto fills in many details of Gileadean history and the organization of the child-bearing system of Handmaids. He reaches no firm conclusion as to Offred's ultimate fate, although his suggestion that she made her way safely to Canada, and possibly to England, seems plausible.

Chapter Five

Specialized vocabulary for the novel

Angels: military fighting men, at war maintaining the borders of the Republic of Gilead. Their full title is "Angels of the Apocalypse."

Aunts: older women who are the custodians, teachers and disciplinarians in charge of the young women conscripted to be Handmaids. They use electric cattle prods to enforce strict rules of conduct.

Birth Day: ritualistic occasion for Handmaids and Wives at the home of a Commander whose Handmaid is about to give birth. The women participate symbolically, the Handmaids as "coaches" during labor, and the Wives as witnesses and celebrants when a healthy, normal child is born and presented to the Commander's Wife as her own.

Birthmobile: a transport vehicle, either red (for Handmaids) or blue (for Wives) that carries women to the home of a Commander whose Handmaid is about to give birth.

Ceremony: a formalized religious service held monthly. The first part, for all members of the household, includes Bible readings and prayers led by the Commander. The second part, in the privacy of the Wife's bedroom, has the Commander and Handmaid performing ritualized sexual intercourse, while the Wife is present in a symbolic role.

Children of Ham: African-Americans who are resettled to farming communities known as the Homelands. The name is an allusion to an incident in the Bible (Genesis 5:20–27). Ham, son of Noah, was cursed by his father for shameful conduct. A later legend developed that Ham became the ancestor of black-skinned people in Africa, who were condemned to be servants. The biblical passage is sometimes cited by white supremacists as justification for their racist beliefs.

Colonies: areas in Gilead where "portable populations" of Unwomen, Gender Traitors and other victims of totalitarian rule live out their few remaining years cleaning up toxic waste sites or disposing of military casualties.

Computers: Several terms in the novel suggest wide use in Gilead of computer technology, usually for close scrutiny of individuals. Examples are Compuchek, a security computer used by barrier guards for checking I.D. and Computalk, an electronic communications terminal.

Econowives: working-class women, who, unlike the Commanders' Wives, have no servants and do everything for themselves.

Eyes: secret police. Their full title is "Eyes of God," alluding to the passage quoted in the Ceremony from II Chronicles 16:9 – "For the eyes of the Lord run to and fro throughout the whole earth, to know himself strong in the behalf of them whose heart is perfect towards him."

Gender Traitor, Gender Treachery: homosexual, homosexuality. Although some Gender Traitors are executed in Gilead, many are sent to the Colonies where they are dressed in gray Unwoman habits and forced to work at cleaning up toxic waste or disposing of military casualties.

Gilead, Republic of: a totalitarian country, formerly the United States, controlled by a military-religious oligarchy. In the Bible, Gilead is an area noted for its fertile pastures, vineyards and olive groves. Atwood's choice of the name is ironic.

Gileadean Research Association: a group sponsoring the university conference in 2195, mentioned in the "Historical Notes" that provide the novel's frame story.

Guardians: armed male guards who carry out domestic policing duties and menial tasks and serve as special aides for privileged Commanders and their Wives. According to Offred, they are "either stupid or older or disabled or very young, apart from the ones [like Nick?] that are Eyes incognito" (p. 25). Their full title is "Guardians of the Faith."

Gyn Ed.: Gynecological Education, the study of female physiological functions and diseases, especially those associated with the reproductive system. Aunt Elizabeth was Offred's instructor in Gyn Ed. at the Red Center.

Identipass: identification papers, required from the earliest days of Gilead, for passing road barriers manned by armed Guardians. Because of the rumored threat from Islamic extremists, everyone approved of the heightened security at first. Then the Identipasses became a requirement imposed by the oppressive authorities in the new restrictions for controlling the populace.

Jewish boat-persons: Jews who were allowed to emigrate to Israel in the early years of Gilead. This repatriation scheme was turned over to private commercial interests, and several boatloads of emigrants were "dumped into the Atlantic, to maximize profits" (p. 383).

Manhattan Cleanup: an incident in the early years of Gilead, typical of many anti-pornography demonstrations in American cities. In New York's Times Square, chanting crowds destroyed sexually alluring female clothing in bonfires, while manufacturers and salesmen of such articles publicly repented on their knees, wearing conical dunce caps marked "SHAME."

Martha: a woman in household service in the Republic of Gilead. In the New Testament gospels of Luke and John, Martha figures in the story of her brother Lazarus, whom Jesus raised from the dead. Martha came to be represented in church art as the patron saint of good housewives, holding household keys and a pot or ladle to signify her service in the kitchen.

Mayday: name of an underground group organized to help escaping Handmaids out of Gilead. The name derives from a twentieth-century international distress call, originally French, *M'aidez*.

National Homeland One: farming area in North Dakota where "Children of Ham" are being resettled to work the land.

Particicution: execution carried out by Handmaids, who are encouraged in their extreme anger and hatred to attack and tear apart a living victim. The word derives from "participation" and "execution."

President's Day Massacre: event that began the revolutionary coup that established the Republic of Gilead. Following a plan developed in the secret Sons of Jacob Think Tanks, right-wing troops shot the U.S. President and machine-gunned members of Congress. The army declared a state of emergency, blaming the massacre on Islamic fanatics. The new military power then began to introduce laws and restrictions for control of the populace.

Pornomarts: retail outlets for the sale of pornography and sexually provocative clothing. The feminists opposed the degradation of women inherent in the sex trade, as did the religious fundamentalists who established Gilead. The latter closed down the Pornomarts, as well as the **Feels-on-Wheels** vans and **Bun-Dle Buggies** (mobile brothels?) soon after seizing power.

Prayvaganza: prayer extravaganza with required attendance of those concerned. There are city-wide, as well as district Prayvaganzas. Those for men only celebrate military victories. The one Offred describes is for women only and is a group wedding of Angels, home from military service, and girls or young women who are given in marriage by the Wives. Other Women's Prayvaganzas are for nuns who recant and take the red veil of the Handmaids.

Red Center: former high school, now serving as indoctrination center and dormitory for Handmaids in training, run by the Aunts. Its correct name is the "Rachel and Leah Re-education Center." The less formal "Red" Center refers ironically to the symbolic color worn by the Handmaids.

Salvaging: public execution ceremony, held separately for men and women. Victims' bodies are then hung on the Wall as warnings to the populace. The word is ironic, suggesting both *salvation*, meaning "rescue," and *savage*, meaning "brutal, inhuman." The Gileadean religious authorities may claim they are rescuing the condemned criminals from their sins, but public execution is an inhuman way to do so.

Save the Women Societies: groups in England who, during the early period of Gilead, assisted escaping Handmaids and others. Records and accounts of daily life in Gilead were used by these groups as propaganda against the Gileadean regime. Offred's memoir may have been intended for their use.

Shredder: a baby born with some external or internal deformation, and subsequently destroyed; also called an "Unbaby." A **keeper** is a healthy baby, born to a Handmaid and given up to be raised by her Commander's Wife.

Sons of Jacob Think Tanks: top secret meetings where the original architects of the revolution and the Gileadean social structure planned the overthrow of the U.S. government. The term "Sons of Jacob" also applied to Jews who, in the early period, were given the chance to convert to approved Christianity, or emigrate to Israel.

Soul Scrolls: a computerized print shop where loyal and devout citizens purchase repeating prayers – printed on recycled paper rolls – for "health, wealth, a death, a birth, a sin" (p. 209). The machines also recite the prayers in metallic voices, a humming murmur through the shop window that suggests the sound of supplicants praying on their knees.

Spheres of Influence Accord: a classified agreement among superpowers that had reached a stalemate in their efforts to control the arms race in the 1970s. The Accord left them free to deal with their own internal rebellions, unhampered by outside interference. The Accord is explained in the "Historical Notes."

Testifying: a self-accusing ritual at the Red Center, whereby a Handmaid publicly confesses to supposed sexual sins – in the case of Janine, for example, to gang-rape and abortion. Testifying is based on fundamentalist Christian practice of telling how one has given up sin and been "born again."

Time Before: our time; the recent time before the revolution that established the Republic of Gilead. Offred recalls in many brief flashbacks details of her own life up to her marriage to Luke and their failed attempt to escape with their five-year-old daughter.

Think Tanks: see "Sons of Jacob."

Unbaby: see "Shredder."

Underground Femaleroad: a series of safe houses operated by subversive groups to help women in escaping Gilead. These way stations are in the homes of religious non-conformists, such as Quakers, and each is in touch only with the next in line. The idea and name derives from the "Underground Railroad" that helped

African-Americans escape slavery in the southern U.S. during the nineteenth century.

Unwomen: women who have, for various reasons, been sent to the Colonies for service in the "portable populations," cleaning up toxic waste and disposing of military casualties. They are women who have no other useful function in society: Handmaids who are unable to conceive or bear healthy, normal children, and older women past child-bearing age.

The Wall: a high, red brick barrier on which the bodies of executed criminals are hung as public warnings to the general populace. Beyond the Wall is the former Harvard University campus, now the headquarters of the secret police, the Eyes, where torture and executions are carried out.

The War: a continuing effort by Gileadean military forces, the Angels, to defend the front lines of the Republic against rebel guerrilla groups. It is impossible for Offred to judge the truth of the biased reports she occasionally sees on television or hears while on shopping excursions. Propaganda and careful control of the media are features of totalitarian rule in Gilead.

Chapter Six

Chapter summaries and commentaries

Note: References are to Margaret Atwood, *The Handmaid's Tale*. Seal Books, McClelland & Stewart Ltd., 1986.

Epigraphs

Summary

Genesis 30: 1-3: The story of Jacob and Rachel is from the Old Testament Book of *Genesis*. To win the hand of Rachel, Jacob worked for her father Laban for seven years but was then given Rachel's less attractive sister Leah as his wife. Leah bore several sons, while Jacob served another seven years to win his beloved Rachel. When Rachel seemed unable to have children, she instructed Jacob to take her handmaid, Bilhah, as a substitute for herself in bearing more children. Eventually, Jacob became father to twelve sons (including two by Rachel), who were the founders of the twelve tribes of Israel.

Jonathan Swift, *A Modest Proposal*: In his satirical pamphlet, published in 1729, Swift mockingly insisted that the extreme poverty of the Irish people might be relieved if they were to raise children as meat products, to be killed and sold as food for the British upper class. Swift even suggested recipes and analyzed the economic advantages his proposal would bring to his impoverished country.

Sufi proverb: The Sufis were an Islamic mystical sect, originating in the seventh century. The Sufi proverb quoted by Atwood is a typical, paradoxical turn of phrase, whose meaning requires careful consideration. In the desert, there is little that might provide nourishment. Wayfarers are free to eat stones if they wish, but no one would expect to get nourishment from stones.

Commentary

- Margaret Atwood uses the epigraphs to prepare us for the **form** and, to some extent, the **theme** of the story to follow. It will be a **narrative** based in part on a Biblical incident. The story will involve surrogate parentage. A major theme will be the exploitation of lower servants to support privileged rulers. This is the basis for the role of the Handmaids in Atwood's novel. The Handmaids produce children as surrogates for the Wives, who take part only symbolically in the actual conception and delivery of babies.

- The tone will be **satirical**, using the portrayal of an extreme form of the future, a post-revolutionary social structure, to depict potential abuses and dangers in contemporary society. Swift's *Modest Proposal* was an eighteenth-century satirical masterpiece, an ironic and bitter criticism of contemporary social theory in Ireland. Margaret Atwood's use of Swift's words signals to the reader that she, too, is writing satire. Her book will look at perceived oppression by a thoughtless and inhumane ruling class.

- The novel's **theme**, its **argument** or **meaning**, is suggested by the Sufi proverb. Like the desert, the Republic of Gilead offers nothing to sustain the human body and spirit. Yet perhaps even the "stones" may, through faith and hope, be transformed into "bread" of spiritual nourishment. The indomitable human spirit can survive even the harshest forms of oppression and persecution.

PART I • NIGHT • Chapter 1

Summary

The narrator describes the dormitory, once a high school gymnasium, where she and other young women (the Handmaids) sleep. She imagines the sports and dances once held in the gym, and recalls the feelings of her generation of teenagers, indulging in sex-play while anxiously longing for the future. That future, the novel's present, is now upon her – a regimented army-cot dormitory. The rows of young women in their beds are separated by spaces. They are not allowed to talk, and their lives are patrolled by Aunt Sara and Aunt Elizabeth, who carry electric cattle-prods as disciplinary weapons. Twice each day, the young women are allowed out for supervised walks around what was once the school's football field, now enclosed by a chain-link fence topped with barbed wire. The dormitory is patrolled by armed guards known as Angels.

Commentary

- Our introduction to the society of the Republic of Gilead is quiet, almost silent. The narrator, whose name is later revealed as Offred, provides enough details of her past to suggest an ordinary adolescence in the 1970s, but the memories are muted, dreamlike, fading in the harsh, austere and empty world she now inhabits.
- The world of her oppression is unexplained, but the physical details are clear: carefully controlled and supervised daily routine, always under threat of punishment for misbehavior, and insulated by armed guards from any outside influence or interference.
- Nevertheless, the narrator and the other young women use secret methods to maintain human contact, sustaining their spirits even under the strict controls of the oppressive system.

Margaret Atwood's literary technique

- **First-person narration:** we see and hear only what the narrator experiences or thinks about. This limited focus creates a strong sense of unity in characterization and plot. However, many questions arise. For example, are the narrator's comments on other characters valid? Is her interpretation of events accurate?
- **Foreshadowing:** through the narrator's limited point of view, the author provides hints and clues about unresolved questions and plot details.

PART II • SHOPPING • Chapter 2

Summary

In the home of the Commander and his Wife, the narrator's room is quite basic. The furnishings – bed, chair, table, lamp, braided rag rug – are old-fashioned, suggestive of "traditional values."

At a bell's signal, Offred prepares to go out. She wears her standard attire: red shoes, red gloves, red cloak and a voluminous red dress with white "wings" screening the sides of her face. She enters the kitchen where Rita, one of the "Marthas," is making bread. Offred recalls eavesdropping once outside a closed door, hearing Rita and another servant, Cora, talking about her own role in the household. She imagines being closer to Rita and Cora, sharing their gossip, instead of being treated by them as an unwelcome but necessary outsider. She thinks of the word "fraternize," and recalls her husband Luke in "the time before," who had a scholar's interest in language, a pedantic interest that she used to tease him about.

Rita gives Offred food tokens to exchange for eggs, cheese and meat on her shopping excursion. She warns Offred to insist on fresh eggs and a young chicken and to remind the food suppliers whose household these supplies are for.

Commentary

- The social structure of the household is a microcosm of the larger society, a hierarchical system from the Commander at the top, down to servants at the bottom. Measures to prevent suicide suggest how oppressive the system must be for those in the Handmaid's position. There are hints about special privileges for those in power.

- Offred's thoughts reveal her character: her warmth, her intelligence, her resolve. "There's a lot that doesn't bear thinking about," she tells us. "Thinking can hurt your chances, and I intend to last" (p. 8). She longs for human contact but has learned to be careful about her survival. She is aware of the symbolism involved in her role as Handmaid, particularly the color red – the color of blood, of birth and new life even in this oppressive society.

- **Foreshadowing:** The role of the Handmaid gives hints about the importance of pregnancy and birth. The potential for violence in this strictly controlled society is suggested. Questions arise whether any individual freedom survives in Gilead. The brief reference to Luke (whose identity is not clear) makes us curious about the narrator's past.

Chapter 3

Summary

As she leaves by the back door, Offred wonders where the Commander's Wife might be and worries about coming upon her unexpectedly. She imagines her in her sitting room, her arthritic left leg propped on a footstool, perhaps knitting scarves for the Angels.

Five weeks earlier, Offred met the Commander's Wife for the first time. She was an older woman dressed in powder-blue robe, wearing large diamonds on her left hand, which rested on the ivory head of her cane. Her cigarettes suggested dealings in the black market, and Offred at first allowed herself to hope that she might be one to bend the rules. She seemed vaguely familiar.

The Commander's Wife made it very clear from the start who was in charge, reminding Offred that in this, her third posting as Handmaid, Offred's position was a little shaky. The less the two women saw of each other, the better. Offred was disappointed, hoping that a closer relationship might have developed. The Commander's Wife also warned that the Commander was *her* husband: "Till death do us part. It's final" (p. 19). Offred knew she could be punished for misbehaving or causing trouble.

Offred suddenly remembered who the Commander's Wife was. She had once been a television personality back when the narrator was eight or nine years old – a singer named Serena Joy on a Sunday morning children's Gospel Hour. The narrator's conclusion was that her new posting might be worse than expected.

Commentary

- This chapter provides more clues about the structure of Gilead society. The Commanders' Wives, for example, have power over the servants. The Wife decides whether the Handmaid is allowed entry by the front door and may inflict physical punishment by "Scriptural precedent." But the Wives' role is limited. Their days are spent in time-filling occupations, tending gardens and knitting.

- Several details about the past emerge. The uncertain status of the Handmaids in these unsettled times suggests that the political coup that created this Gilead was quite recent. In regard to personal interests, Offred tells us that she once had a garden. Her love of the physical sensations, the smell of earth and the textures of bulbs and seeds, suggests how she once enjoyed such simple human pleasures. Her troubling memory of the Commander's Wife as Serena Joy, a former television evangelist, is another hint about a strong religious element in Gilead's suppression of individual freedoms.

Chapter 4

Summary

The narrator sets out on her shopping excursion, passing a Guardian named Nick, the chauffeur, who is washing the Commander's expensive car. Offred imagines being close to the chauffeur, aware of his body and smell, but she worries that he might be an Eye, a member of the secret police.

At the street corner, Offred meets her shopping companion, a Handmaid named Ofglen. Shopping in pairs makes each Handmaid a spy on her companion's behavior. They walk along, commenting on the ongoing war and recent persecutions of religious dissidents. They pass barriers where green-uniformed Guardians of the Faith stamp their identification passes. When one young Guardian sneaks a look at Offred, she feels she would like to touch his youthful face and imagines coming to him secretly at night.

She briefly mentions, without explanation, several features of this oppressive society, such as Salvagings, Prayvaganzas and the Birthmobile. She also describes sinister vans, with winged white Eyes painted on their black sides, and dark-tinted windows. For illicit nighttime meetings, there may be sudden floodlights, rifle shots. Perhaps the young Guardians at the barricades think only of duty, and of promotion to the Angels. Nevertheless, as they pass the barrier, aware of the young Guardians' gaze, Offred allows herself a small indulgence, a movement of her hips that makes her red dress sway, teasing the young men with what they cannot have.

Commentary

- Chapter 4 suggests the importance of the military and reveals how young Guardians, not yet assigned to the army, provide necessary policing services. Some, like Nick, may be assigned to important households. Again, we are aware of sinister control by the secret police.

- Offred is under constant observation. Nevertheless, she has enough independence of character still to allow herself minor indiscretions, such as teasing the young Guardians who stamp her identity papers. This incident shows Offred taking minor risks, defying convention in order to maintain her individuality, her sense of self.

• Offred's repressed sexuality becomes more apparent, in her awareness of Nick's physical presence and in her teasing of the young Guardians at the checkpoint by swaying her hips provocatively as she passes through.

Chapter 5

Summary

Walking through her affluent neighborhood, Offred recalls strolling there with Luke, thinking about a home and family. On the main street, she again recalls the past, as a child roaming the city, and later as an adult aware of increasing threats of violence. Aunt Lydia at the Red Center spoke of two kinds of freedom: in the time before, "freedom to" do what one wanted; and now, "freedom from" fear, intimidation, violence.

The shops have appropriate names for a religion-dominated society. A clothing store called "Lilies of the Field" sells the Handmaids' red dresses, styled like the habits of nuns in the time before. In the store called "Milk and Honey," Offred exchanges tokens for milk and eggs. She hopes she might see someone she knows, perhaps her college friend Moira. Two Handmaids enter, and one of them, called Ofwarren, is clearly pregnant. Offred recognizes her as Janine, one of Aunt Lydia's pets.

At "All Flesh" they collect paper-wrapped parcels of meat and chicken. Again Offred recalls the past, how she worried that her infant daughter might accidentally suffocate while playing with plastic shopping bags – but she blocks such thoughts: they are too private, too revealing of her inner life.

On the street again, Offred and Ofglen are confronted by a group of Japanese tourists. The women's clothes and make-up are of the old days. The Handmaids are fascinated, but their Red Center indoctrination also makes them feel repelled. When the tourists ask if the strange, red-clad Handmaids are happy, Offred – knowing that silence can sometimes be dangerous – feels compelled to say, "Yes, we are very happy."

Commentary

- Chapter 5 fills in more details of the oppressive society. In the upscale neighborhood, the absence of children illustrates the bleak and empty routine of the inhabitants' lives. The pervasiveness of religion is apparent in simple things such as the names of shops, each an appropriate biblical allusion. An incident with Asian tourists provides a stunning contrast between women's clothing styles of the past, and the compulsory, nun-like coverings of the Handmaids.

- The incident concerning Ofwarren, formerly known as Janine, flaunting her success in the child-bearing process, **foreshadows** a major episode to come. We are gradually learning the importance of the Handmaids, through hints about their roles as surrogates for the Commanders' childless Wives.

- Brief flashbacks are often simple associations Offred makes, scenic fragments of her past world contrasting with her present situation. For example, the clothing shop, located in what was once a movie theater, prompts Offred's memories of old films with strong female characters. They had the power to choose, Offred thinks, implying that in her present life, personal choices are few. Aunt Lydia at the Red Center, whose teachings Offred sometimes mocks, seems to have had a relevant comment for every situation. Regarding "choice," Aunt Lydia once stated that society was "dying . . . of too much choice" (p. 31), implying the Handmaids are much better off when choices are restricted.

Chapter 6

Summary

Ofglen suggests she and Offred return by way of the Wall. There, six hooded bodies hang from large hooks mounted on the brickwork, victims of executions carried out the same morning at a Salvaging ceremony. White lab coats and identifying placards indicate they were doctors who performed abortions in the time before. Now, exposed and executed, they are frightening examples to others. No matter that their actions were once legal, Offred says. "Their crimes are retroactive" (p. 42), atrocities to be punished under the new social order. Offred feels no hatred or scorn for these men, but only relief that none of them is Luke. However, she wonders what emotions Ofglen, who seems to tremble beside her, might be suppressing.

Commentary

- Hints about the novel's **setting** indicate that Offred's world is part of a university campus (Harvard, in Cambridge, Massachusetts), where former dormitories, a football stadium and a riverside boathouse suggest under-graduate activities of the past. A subway linking the campus to the "main city" (Boston) is now travelled only by those with official permission. Harsh oppression enforced by those in control is obvious in the scene at the Wall. Here victims of a witch hunt are exposed to public view.

- We gain further insight into Offred's character. In her mind, she criticizes and condemns abuses around her, although her public attitudes and activities conform to accepted rules. She discovers Ofglen is much like herself: the image of public conformity masks her private, inner life and identity.

Retroactive crimes

Offred says of the executed abortion doctors, "Their crimes are retroactive."

• Retroactive ("applying to the past as well as to the present and future") here refers to activities (abortions) now prosecuted as crimes, which were not considered illegal at the time they were performed, before the Gileadean coup.

• One of the basic rights of democracy is protection against such abuses of the legal system, but they are common practice under totalitarian rule.

PART III • NIGHT • Chapter 7

Summary

Alone in her room, Offred looks among her memories for "somewhere good" to go. First, she recalls university studies with her friend Moira. Then she remembers a much earlier time, when she was about five. On a cold Saturday, her mother met with activist friends who were publicly burning pornographic magazines. Young Offred, innocent of the event's implications, threw a magazine on the flames.

Then Offred tries to remember the traumatic "lost time," after her daughter was taken from her. Those in charge showed her a photograph of the child in good hands – an angel in white, beside a woman unknown to Offred.

Offred wishes her story – the book we are reading – were just fiction, the ending of which she controls. Believing her story is only fiction would give her a better chance of surviving, she thinks. If she can control the ending, then she may eventually reunite with her husband and daughter. But she knows her present life is not a fiction. She can only pretend, vaguely and with little real hope, that she will survive and that someone will someday hear her story.

Commentary

• This interlude briefly introduces two important influences in Offred's life: Moira and her mother. Offred recalls some memories with pleasure, but she is also haunted by images difficult to face. The book-burning incident brings up feminist issues of the 1960s, which were her mother's concern, and are now, by implication, her own. The incident involving Offred's daughter raises more questions about how and why Gilead was established.

PART IV • WAITING ROOM • Chapter 8

Summary

On a later excursion, Ofglen comments on this "beautiful May day" (p. 54), and Offred thinks back to Luke's explanation of the wartime distress call, "Mayday": from French, *m'aidez*, meaning "Help me."

Then the two women witness a funeral procession. The Handmaids show appropriate respect for the bereaved mother of a miscarried fetus, but one of the Econowives demonstrates her dislike of the Handmaids by spitting as she passes. When Offred and Ofglen take formal leave of each other, Ofglen hesitates briefly, as if to say something more, then turns and walks away.

At home, Nick is polishing the Commander's car. He greets Offred, although he is not supposed to speak to her. Offred recalls Aunt Lydia's statement that men are weak. It is up to the women to establish "boundaries."

When Offred sees the Commander's Wife sitting among her tulips, she recalls an old magazine article. Serena Joy had sacrificed her domestic life to make public speeches about the sanctity of the home. Feminist and anti-feminist groups were clashing at the time, and there had even been attempts to assassinate her. Now Offred imagines the Wife must be furious, forced to live an influential but barren life as mistress of this household. She recalls Aunt Lydia's appeal to the Handmaids to try to understand and sympathize with the Wives, these "defeated" women.

In the kitchen, Rita comments on the scrawny chicken Offred has brought. Cora, the younger Martha, agrees to help prepare for Offred's bath night. In the upstairs hallway, Offred is suddenly confronted by the Commander. He is violating custom by gazing into her room, a part of the house where he is not supposed to be. He passes her, showing the required respect but without speaking. This leaves Offred puzzled.

Commentary

- New details emerge regarding Gilead: routine execution of members of outlawed religious sects and sexual deviants. The coded reference to "Mayday" hints there may be an underground movement fed by social unrest; but so far, Offred appears to have no suspicion of this possibility.
- Offred's memories of Aunt Lydia bring up the feminist issues that are a central **theme**. Aunt Lydia's comment on the weakness of men suggests that women must maintain a strong influence in home and family life, by setting boundaries in their relations with others in the household.

- Feminist issues also form part of the historical background. Serena Joy, once the anti-feminist public figure pleading for family values and traditional women's roles, is now a prisoner of the very lifestyle she once crusaded for. The irony is emphasized here.

- The approaching bath night foreshadows a major episode, the ritualistic mating Ceremony that will dominate Chapters 14 to 16. This chapter ends with a puzzling incident: our first in-person encounter with the Commander outside Offred's room.

- Symbolism abounds in this novel, and a major symbol is suggested here. Traditionally, a room is a feminine symbol, a "womb," a private space where any male influence must be considered an intrusion. The title of this section (chs. 8–12) is "Waiting Room." Symbolically, Offred *is* the waiting room, a waiting *womb*, waiting for the kind of fulfilment Gileadean society demands of her. Thus, the Commander's brief intrusion foreshadows coming events in the Ceremony. Meanwhile, Offred also waits in the privacy of her inner self, her inner "room," for events to happen that will get her through this story to reconnect with her former life.

Chapter 9

Summary

As she waits, Offred thinks about the previous Handmaid whose existence she had discovered when exploring her room three days after arriving. She also recalls incidents back in the mid-1970s, before she and Luke were married, in hotel rooms where they carried on their secret affair. She thinks how careless she was then about the freedom and happiness involved in ordinary things that now seem impossible.

In the early days of her present posting, she examined her room very carefully, noting signs that two people had once made love here. She also became aware that a chandelier hook had been removed from the ceiling, and she knew why the window had shatter-proof glass. In examining the cupboard, she discovered scratched words: *Nolite te bastardes carborundorum*. Offred guessed the phrase was

Latin, which she does not know, a message left by the previous Handmaid. She was pleased to feel this contact with the woman and imagined her to be like her college friend Moira: young, athletic, resourceful. When Offred asked Rita about her predecessor, the cook would say only that she had not worked out.

Commentary

- The missing chandelier hook and the shatterproof window glass illustrate the oppressive nature of Gilead. Suicide must be tempting for those forced to suffer the stifling restraints of the Handmaid's role.

- In her **limited point of view**, Offred misses (for now) the meaning of the Latin inscription: *Don't let the bastards grind you down*. Its attraction confirms her need for contact with others who share her situation. We can look forward to a time when the message, translated, will give Offred courage in her struggle.

CHAPTER 10

Summary

Offred, waiting, sometimes recalls old songs, outlawed hymns or Elvis Presley tunes. She recalls Aunt Lydia speaking of the immorality of the time before, and vowing, despite her own feelings, to do her best for the women training as Handmaids.

Offred recalls her friend Moira, who was a strong supporter of the feminist movement while anti-feminist outrages – rape and murder – became increasingly common. Offred muses on how the backlash against feminists gradually developed.

She hears the Commander's car in the driveway, and sits at her window. She wonders whether reading one word – "FAITH" stitched on a small cushion – would count as a crime. Below in the driveway, she sees Nick and the Commander. She imagines spitting out the window or throwing the cushion to hit the Commander. This evokes another memory of college, when she and Moira water-bombed male students during a panty-raid.

She watches the Commander leave in his car. She thinks she ought to hate him, but does not. Her feelings about him are more complicated.

Commentary

- Further restrictions on individual behavior are revealed, such as the prohibitions against believing in a personal God, or loving and being heartbroken. Aunt Lydia contrasts the immoral freedoms of the past with the present. The forbidden act of reading also contrasts with a time when Offred and Moira enjoyed independence at university, being involved in the feminist movement and indulging in harmless pranks.

- Offred's present feelings about the Commander are unclear. She knows how she should feel, hating him for her subservient role in his household. But she is confused by his odd behavior outside her room and can only wait, perhaps to take advantage of coming events.

Chapter 11

Summary

Offred describes her most recent visit to a doctor, an obligatory monthly medical checkup for Handmaids. In the waiting room, Offred and two other Handmaids covertly size up each other, looking for signs of pregnancy, while the nurse checks identities in his computer files.

In the examination room, Offred arranges herself on the table so that the doctor sees her body only from the neck down. Breaking the rules, he chats as he examines her, calling her "honey" and touching her leg. He lifts the sheet to look at her face and whispers a proposition, offering to "help" her, to make her pregnant. He comments that the Commanders are often too old, that some are sterile (unable to have children).

Offred knows the power the doctor holds – power to have her shipped to the Colonies as an Unwoman. But she is frightened by the death penalty if they are caught. She declines his offer without offending him, but he suggests she might reconsider before her next visit.

As she dresses, Offred, hands shaking, wonders about her fear. The thought of having a choice, a way out of her situation, is terrifying.

- This brief episode reveals the way some men in positions of trust secretly defy society's strict controls. Although the doctor says he wants to help Offred, his unstated motive may be simple sexual desire. He is, no doubt, as conscious as Offred of the possibilities of blackmail.

- The risks of satisfying personal choice is a **thematic thread** that runs through the novel. According to Aunt Lydia, society in the time before was "dying of too much choice" (p. 31), but now life without choice has become "ordinary" (another of Aunt Lydia's comments on the strength of society's rules and controls, p. 43).

Here Offred is given a terrifying choice: to continue in her law-abiding, subservient role; or to rebel against Gilead's stringent restrictions and allow the doctor to "help" her to a position of respect.

Chapter 12

Summary

Offred's bath night is a luxury, as well as a social requirement before the Ceremony. The warm water and the smell of soap trigger a memory of her daughter. Offred remembers a Saturday with Luke, when a woman tried to steal the one-year-old child from a supermarket shopping cart. Then she imagines her at the age of five, taken by the authorities. Offred remembers photographs of them together. Then she sees herself alone, beside an open drawer or trunk where baby clothes were carefully put away with a treasured lock of hair. Those things are gone now. Offred wonders whether her little girl is still alive. She would be eight years old.

Cora interrupts, insisting that Offred finish quickly. She soaps and scrubs carefully, knowing she will not be able to wash again after tonight's Ceremony. She notes the small tattoo on her ankle – the eye symbol and four-digit identification number.

Back in her room she dresses in fresh clothes. Cora knocks before entering with supper, a well-balanced selection of chicken, vegetables, salad and canned pears. Here in the heartland of Gilead, the Handmaids lead a pampered life, according to Aunt Lydia; but this evening Offred finds eating difficult. With no way to get rid of the food secretly, she forces herself to eat. She imagines the elegant dinner table downstairs. Perhaps Serena Joy has also lost her appetite, but simply leaves her food uneaten.

Offred tears off part of her paper napkin and wraps a pat of butter in it. She hides this in a shoe in the bottom of the cupboard, to be used later. She then composes herself to wait.

Commentary

- Background information on the dystopian **setting** is revealed. For example, the fear that alert spies will spot any deviation from the accepted norm, is a fact of life. Even the private luxury of a warm bath may be abruptly interrupted.

- From various clues, we can now outline Offred's life story and understand her feelings about the past. The most traumatic incident was the removal of her five-year-old child, and even the few mementos Offred once treasured were confiscated by the authorities.

- The secret pat of butter in her shoe is, for now, puzzling. Meanwhile we wait, perhaps just as nervously as Offred, for the Ceremony and its significance to be revealed and explained.

Time line:
Offred in the time before

Margaret Atwood suggests these approximate dates by reference to current events in the real world.

c. 1960 Offred, as a child about five years old, takes part in feminist book-burning with her mother

c. 1975 Offred and Moira at university

c. 1978 Offred's secret affair with married Luke

c. 1980 Offred and Luke married with baby daughter; attempted abduction of child by stranger

c. 1983 Revolution establishes Republic of Gilead; new laws, close restrictions, limitations on personal freedom

c. 1985 Offred and Luke attempt escape to Canada; Luke possibly killed or captured; daughter five years old, taken by authorities; Offred's traumatic "lost time"

c. 1986 Offred, Moira, Janine at Re-Education Center

c. 1988 Offred's third posting as Handmaid, to household of Commander Fred and Serena Joy

PART V • NAP • Chapter 13

Summary

As Offred waits for the evening Ceremony, she goes through an exercise routine learned at the Red Center. She recalls afternoon naps there, and suspects the Handmaids were sedated with drugs in their food to keep them calm. Three weeks after her own arrival at the Red Center, her college friend Moira appeared. They had met secretly in the washroom and exchanged a few words.

Offred describes a session of Testifying, when a Handmaid would reveal something personally shameful, to be subject to public mockery and humiliation. When Janine testified about a gang-rape and subsequent abortion when she was fourteen, Aunt Lydia emphasized that she was at fault for leading on her attackers; God's purpose was to teach her a lesson. Although Offred felt mean-spirited about doing so, she joined in the chanted cries of blame and mockery directed at Janine.

Offred is dreaming now, about a time when she and Luke were first married. The dream is troubling, and Offred fears that Luke might be dead. She sees herself running with her five-year-old daughter through autumn woods, trying to escape pursuit and the gunshots she hears behind her. Later in the dream she is being restrained, while her child is taken from her.

Offred wakes to the sound of a bell and Cora knocking at her door. "Of all the dreams," she thinks, "this is the worst."

Commentary

- Indoctrination at the Re-Education Center involved physical deprivation and training sessions. Offred also suspects drugs were used to crush their spirits. Testifying meant public humiliation for those who, like Janine, made a good show of their guilt over shameful incidents.
- Dozing off, Offred imagines her whole being in terms of her function in the Commander's household and in society. She experiences life's emptiness in terms of her empty body and edges toward despair as she fruitlessly marks time.

- Offred's memories give both pain and pleasure. At the Red Center, she was ashamed of her behavior when Janine testified. But she happily remembers Moira and their secret friendship. Dreams are not so easily controlled. We learn a few details about married life with Luke, but that dream becomes a nightmare. Their attempted escape from Gilead ends in failure – Offred taken prisoner, her daughter carried off, Luke possibly shot and killed. Offred is determined to survive; but in these waiting times, memories and dreams haunt her.

PART VI • HOUSEHOLD • Chapter 14

Summary
Offred descends to the sitting room and kneels beside Serena Joy's chair. She feels she would like to steal something from this elegantly furnished room. Such a risky act would give her a sense of power. Cora and Rita enter, looking resentful about being interrupted in their chores. Everyone in the household must attend the Ceremony. Nick arrives and stands behind Offred, the toe of his boot just touching the Handmaid's shoe. When she shifts her foot, he moves his to maintain the secret contact.

Serena Joy arrives, commenting on the Commander being "late, as usual." She turns on the television set and changes channels to find a news program. Offred is eager for news of any kind. She knows it may be faked but hopes to "read" the truth behind official propaganda.

The group watch images of military activities, and Offred tries to decipher the face and thoughts of one captured resistance fighter. More news follows, of a conspiracy to smuggle "national resources" into Canada, and columns of smoke against background sounds of military gunfire in what was once Detroit. Then the grandfatherly anchorman announces the resettlement of three thousand Children of Ham to farms in North Dakota. Serena Joy impatiently changes channels, pauses on an aging singer performing an old hymn, and then switches off.

Offred's mind wanders. She thinks about her real name in the past, her secret identity separate from her role as Handmaid. She recalls a September Saturday in the car with Luke, their daughter playing with dolls beside a picnic basket in the back seat. With forged passports and few belongings, they hoped to cross the border as if on a day trip to Canada. Tension grew, and she worried about how they would get past military checkpoints to be safe as a family.

Commentary

- More details of **setting** emerge in this chapter: everyday religious elements, the political and military situation and the importance of propaganda. For the Ceremony, attendance by everyone in the Commander's household is required. Religion is a collective endeavor, requiring obedience, conformity and group "witnessing" to confirm the Ceremony's validity. Religious singers and preachers on television are also important in everyday life. More important to Offred are clues about what really goes on in the world of martial law and the continuing war, behind the government-sponsored propaganda. For example, the resettlement of three thousand so-called "Children of Ham" to a farming area suggests that slavery of African-Americans is once again in practice. A second example involves the smuggling of "precious natural resources" via an "underground railroad," similar to the nineteenth-century operation that guided runaway slaves north. Now the so-called "Underground Femaleroad" carries escaping Handmaids ("precious natural resources") to freedom in Canada.

- Offred's memory of the escape attempt with Luke and their daughter fills in more details of her past. At the time, Offred tells us, fear made her feel incapable of holding on to Luke and her child. Her current struggle to maintain her sense of self and her sanity was foreshadowed years before, with the traumatic, life-changing escape attempt. By imagining Moira's reaction to such thoughts, Offred uses her friend's strength of character as support in her internal conflict.

Chapter 15

Summary
The Commander knocks and enters the sitting room immediately, ignoring protocol. He takes a Bible from a box beside his chair, and begins to read the usual stories of Adam and Noah. As Offred's mind wanders, he begins the story of Jacob's wives.

She recalls similar routines at the Center, such as the reading of biblical passages that had been altered to reflect the special requirements of "re-education." She also recalls a secret meeting when her friend Moira was planning to escape by faking illness. Moira implied that she might try to seduce the Angels assigned to accompany her to hospital.

Offred's attention comes back to the Commander, still reading the story of the handmaid who serves as surrogate mother for Jacob's child by Rachel. Serena Joy is quietly weeping. As the Commander calls for God's blessing on "all our ventures," Offred thinks about how much Serena Joy must hate her for the sexual role she is about to play in the Ceremony's second part.

Offred prays silently, using the Latin phrase, *Nolite te bastardes carborundorum*, even though she does not know its meaning. She thinks again of Moira, remembering how she was taken away by ambulance. When the ambulance returned, Moira, unable to walk, was dragged into the school's former Science Lab. She could not walk for a week, her feet were so swollen. Punishment for a first offense was torture involving steel cables. As Aunt Lydia said, "For our purposes your feet and your hands are not essential" (p. 114).

Offred continues praying, until the Commander ends the session with a final religious injunction about God's strong help for those who try to be perfect for Him.

Commentary
- The meaning of the Ceremony is clarified in this chapter, confirming Offred's role as substitute for Serena Joy in her most important duty: bearing the Commander's children.
- Part of the Handmaids' re-education involves physical torture for breaches of the rules. Moira's brief escape, and her attempted

seduction of the ambulance attendants, results in serious injuries. Aunt Lydia's cold statement about torture illustrates a principle of totalitarian rule: crush individuality and exploit the masses by any expedient means to maintain power at the top.

- Moira's break-out fills in **character** details. Her individuality is not easily crushed. She is a free spirit who takes large risks and endures physical punishment for the sake of personal freedom, no matter how short-lived. She is intelligent, clever and pragmatic, a woman who sees the system's flaws and knows she can exploit them. And she is a sexual woman, thinking in terms of physical satisfaction. No wonder Offred clings to her memories of Moira for strength and support.

Chapter 16

Summary

The Ceremony continues for the Commander, Serena Joy and Offred. The Commander performs a ritualized mating with Offred, who lies on her back, head resting on Serena Joy's pelvis. The Wife holds Offred's raised arms, controlling their symbolically united bodies.

Offred cannot call this ritual "making love" or even "copulating," since these terms are not accurate when only one person, the Commander, is really involved. Nor can she call it "rape," since there is nothing going on that she has not agreed to. She tells us, "There wasn't a lot of choice but there was some, and this is what I chose" (p. 116). The act itself has "nothing to do with passion or love or romance or . . . sexual desire" (p. 117). It is serious business, duty.

The Commander reaches orgasm and immediately leaves. Offred finds the exercise somewhat hilarious but does not dare laugh. Serena Joy quickly orders the Handmaid out, loathing evident in her voice. As she leaves, Offred wonders whether the experience is worse for Serena Joy or for herself.

Commentary

- The low Gileadean birth rate is partly a consequence of environmental pollution. As a result, the bearing of healthy children is of primary concern. The use of biblical precedent (the Rachel and Leah story) to validate the unusual mating ritual illustrates once again the authoritarian control by religious and political leaders. Even the most basic creative energy is exploited by the state.

- Chapters 14 through 16 highlight Serena Joy's **character**. She waits impatiently for the Commander, displaying her cold manner and strict attention to rules of appropriate behavior. She is a stern and commanding figure. Yet when the Commander reads the Rachel and Leah story, Serena Joy weeps, because the biblical tale emphasizes her position as the infertile member of the three-person mating ritual. After the Ceremony, duty done, she rudely dismisses Offred, unable to hide her feelings of loathing toward the Handmaid.

- Both women are demeaned in the Ceremony, where sex and love are reduced to matters of social necessity.

Chapter 17

Summary

In her room, Offred uses the hidden butter (Chapter 12) as skin lotion on her face and hands. At her window, she watches the new moon, and feels symbolic associations with ancient magic. She longs for Luke, to be held by him and called by her former name.

The thought comes again that she wants to steal something. She quietly returns to the sitting room and considers taking a fading flower to press under her mattress as a message to the Handmaid who will follow her. Nick enters, assuring her that she has nothing to fear, but Offred knows their meeting is forbidden and in forbidden territory. He pulls her to him. For a moment they are both tempted to do more than kiss, to fulfill their sexual needs, but reason and fear prevent them.

Nick explains why the Commander has sent him. He wants to see her in his office the next day. As she retreats, Offred is again puzzled and worried by the Commander's unusual attention.

Commentary

- Atwood continues to illustrate contrasting elements in Offred's complex character. We have seen already her resolve to survive and her deep desire to return to her former life. Now she shows she can be humorously critical, while clarifying the real significance of her Handmaid role. In chapter sixteen, she wanted to laugh about the "three-way" sexual ritual despite the seriousness of the Ceremony. Here she enjoys describing herself as "buttered . . . like a piece of toast," knowing she will eventually smell like rancid cheese. The serious thought behind her humor is this: her desire for soft skin means she believes in a future and freedom, a time when Handmaids "will be touched again, in love or desire" (p. 121). Private rituals are important to Offred's survival instinct, and show her strength and continuing courage.

- So far in this novel, **plot** has been relatively unimportant. Memories of the time before serve to illustrate character and suggest how Offred came to her present situation. Incidents in the present, such as shopping excursions and the Ceremony, illustrate features of society, oppressive laws and rules for individual conduct both public and private. Now we are given a clear beginning to a plot line that will develop into a conflict beyond Offred's internal struggle. The Commander's special attention to Offred foreshadows secret, perhaps subversive developments in the Handmaid's story.

- The forbidden lust of Nick, and later of the Commander, continues the theme of repressed sexuality in Gilead.

Contending forces in fictional dystopia

In dystopian fiction, the "ideal" state is founded on totalitarian and oppressive measures, enforced to keep the majority of the population in carefully controlled restraints. Usually the creator of a fictional dystopia also lets us see the subversive elements that threaten the stability and efficiency of government and society.

In The Handmaid's Tale, *Margaret Atwood allows her readers to observe and understand both sides, more than the average citizen can know. Sometimes we see more than her central character – the narrator, Offred – fully understands.*

Methods of control:

- To maintain its existence, the Republic of Gilead requires secret police (the "Eyes"), armed Guardians, ongoing military defense of its borders, and cruel persecution of non-conforming religious groups, free-thinking medical personnel and feminists.
- Indoctrination of the Handmaids at the "Re-education Center" is based on endless repetition of religious precepts and rules for behavior, fear of punishment and personal humiliation – all of which amount to brain-washing.
- Sexual activity is serious business, intended only to repopulate the state with healthy children. Ritualized sex is strictly controlled by military enforcement and religious precept.

Elements of subversion:

- Those at the top exploit the system, using their powerful positions to enjoy special privileges, such as private chauffeurs and the best food supplies.
- A secret economy, the "black market," exists for traffic in forbidden products, such as tobacco and liquor.
- Secret sexual affairs are arranged, even by and for those in command. Later we will learn that prostitution (at "Jezebel's") is also part of the underground scene.
- An "underground railway" is at work, to help escaping fugitives out of Gilead.

PART VII • NIGHT • Chapter 18

Summary

Still trembling after her encounter with Nick, Offred recalls her husband Luke and thinks about her present, loveless situation. She imagines that all the people she loves are dead or otherwise missing, and for them, she is also a missing person. Offred wants someone real to hold, but thinks of her own body as lifeless.

Offred imagines three possibilities about Luke's fate. First she sees him dead in the autumn woods after their attempted escape from Gilead. Then she imagines him a prisoner, looking ten or twenty years older than he should. He has survived and believes her to be alive, too. Finally, she imagines him safe across the border and part of an underground resistance movement. She imagines him contacting her with rescue plans. This image is what keeps her alive. She knows these three possibilities cannot all be true, but somehow holds on to them as an exercise in hope. She will be ready, whatever the truth turns out to be.

Offred recalls a gravestone in the cemetery, engraved with the words "In hope," and the symbols of an anchor and hourglass. She wonders whether "In hope" applies to the corpse or to those still alive. She wonders whether Luke, like her, lives in hope.

Commentary

- This interlude gives us further insight into Offred's inner struggle, her determination to survive. Her first image, of Luke dead, is superseded by the possibility of his survival. The third version dominates, based on hope for a future together.

- Traditional Christian symbols are part of Offred's imaginings. An anchor represents firm hope for, and belief in, everlasting life. The hourglass represents time passing. These symbols provide insight into what dominates Offred's private thoughts: hope for survival and the passage of time that will bring a renewal of life for her and her family.

- Atwood's female characters often think of themselves as lifeless or drowning, a theme evident in much of her poetry as well as her other novels.

PART VIII • BIRTH DAY • Chapter 19

Summary

Offred wakes from troubling dreams of her daughter and of herself as a child. Feeling groggy, she wonders whether her life is a drug-induced delusion. Then reason prevails, and she concludes that such thinking is a test of the sanity she must cling to.

As she prepares to eat her breakfast, Offred finds pleasure in the simplicity of a boiled egg – its shape, its texture, its warmth. Blessings, she thinks, can be simple; then she imagines that this is society's approved way of thinking, and she simply eats the egg.

She hears an approaching siren and sees a red van stop out front. Cora hurries her downstairs and she runs out the front door to the red "Birthmobile." Three Handmaids are already seated in the van. Offred questions one woman and learns that Ofwarren (Janine at the Red Center) is the reason for their excursion. The Handmaids' joy is apparent.

Offred wonders what the result of Ofwarren's pregnancy will be. Because of toxic pollution, there is a 75 per cent chance that a pregnancy carried to full term will result in an "Unbaby" that will be destroyed. Offred imagines her own body, possibly carrying radioactive or biological pollutants. She recalls Aunt Lydia's condemnation of women who prevented pregnancies with pills or by surgical means. Aunt Lydia had assured the Handmaids that despite the risks, their duty was to carry on courageously in repopulating Gilead. Aunt Lydia insisted they should think of themselves as valued "pearls" for their ability to produce children. Offred and the others at the Red Center wondered what became of the Unbabies, the "shredders."

The red Birthmobile stops, and the Handmaids are "herded" out by Guardians. The big Emerge van is there, with medical equipment and doctors available only for emergencies. Offred recalls Aunt Lydia denouncing childbirth in the old way, with anaesthetics and doctors. To Aunt Lydia, the suffering pronounced upon Eve in the Genesis story must be the norm: "in sorrow thou shalt bring forth children" (p. 143).

A blue Birthmobile also drives up, carrying Serena Joy and other local Wives. Offred imagines them visiting here previously, to see pregnant Janine "paraded out." She sarcastically imagines the Wives' gossip, their malicious comments about Handmaids, while Janine upstairs waits, unthinking, to bring credit to Commander Warren's household.

Commentary

- The importance of the Handmaids is highlighted in this chapter. The author cites the poisoned environment for the decline in the birthrate and explains the religious foundation for the Handmaid's duties.

- Janine (Ofwarren) is the central figure in a **subplot**. We first saw her showing off her pregnancy in Chapter 5. In Chapter 13, Offred recalled her at the Red Center, "testifying" and being humiliated. Now she is the pampered surrogate for her Commander's Wife. Later, we will learn more about her, including the results of her pregnancy and its long-lasting effects on her. Janine's story provides a significant contrast to Offred's. The two Handmaids ultimately demonstrate different ways of holding on to a sense of self, to sanity, to hope for a future.

Chapter 20

Summary

Offred notes the lunch preparations for Ofwarren's Birth Day. The Wives themselves have begun their ritualized encouragement of Commander Warren's aging Wife, massaging her thin stomach as if she were the one about to give birth. Meanwhile, Janine, in actual labor, is in the master bedroom, surrounded by Handmaids. Aunt Elizabeth from the Red Center is present, waiting with the two-seater Birthing Stool.

Offred recalls the weekly movies the Aunts showed them at the Red Center. Sometimes they were old pornographic films depicting abnormal sex or the physical mutilation and torture of women. They warned against what might have been the Handmaids' fate if the revolution had not eradicated all such abominations. Sometimes the films were Unwoman documentaries, shown without sound. According to Aunt Lydia, the Unwomen wasted time in their feminist activities, although some of them had good ideas. These women, including Offred's own mother, wearing plaid shirts, jeans and sneakers, demonstrated with banners protesting widespread prostitution and the pornographic exploitation of females. They also campaigned for freedom of choice: to carry a wanted child full term and give birth, or to undergo legal abortion.

Offred recalls conversations with her mother. The spunky, wiry, gray-haired woman liked to visit, drink and complain about life while Offred and Luke fixed dinner. Her attitude about men was simple: "A man is just a woman's strategy for making other women" (p. 151). She and Luke had gotten along well, teasing each other with mock insults. After three drinks, Offred's mother would complain about how little the younger generation understood the feminists' sacrifices, about how lonely she had been despite her female friends.

Offred and her mother sometimes argued more seriously. Offred insisted that she could not be the justification of her mother's choices, representing feminist ideas. She asserted her own independence, her own choices. Nevertheless, Offred now wishes she could have that former life again – arguing with her mother but appreciating her company and even her criticisms.

Commentary

- Through Offred's mother – especially her cynical and satirical comments about men and marriage – Margaret Atwood satirizes the feminist movement of the 1970s and 1980s. The Unwomen documentaries illustrate the Aunts' official position on feminist issues.

- Offred tries to steer a middle course between opposing influences. On one hand, Janine represents the dangers of complete submission. On the other hand, Offred admires and envies the rebellious attitudes of her friend Moira. For now at least, Offred's choice is still HOPE – always vague, never fully articulated – that the present reality will pass. She hopes somehow to return to her former life, when freedom to love her husband and child and to argue with her mother was taken for granted.

Chapter 21

Summary

The Handmaids chant as they have been taught, helping Janine to breathe through her labor contractions. Vicariously, Offred feels the birth pangs. Janine cries out in pain, and Offred recalls her noisy sobbing at the Red Center over the memory of an earlier child she had borne.

Aunt Elizabeth announces that Janine's time has come, and the Wife is sent for. Janine takes her place on the lower seat of the Birthing Stool. Commander Warren's Wife sits behind and above Janine, supported by two of the Wives. The Handmaids continue their routine, chanting "Push, push," feeling as lost in the moment as Janine is. Aunt Elizabeth kneels with a towel, ready to catch the baby. They wait expectantly as Aunt Elizabeth inspects the newborn. When she looks up smiling, satisfied the little girl is normal, all of them cry with joy and share in Janine's success.

The Wife is helped to her bed where the baby is ceremoniously placed in her arms. The other Wives now push into the room with their plates and wine glasses, shoving the Handmaids aside to crowd enviously around. Commander' Warren's Wife officially names the child "Angela," and the twittering Wives approve. Meanwhile, the Handmaids stand around Janine, screening her. She cries helplessly, but Offred says they are all jubilant at the victory they have together accomplished. After nursing the baby for a few months, Janine will be transferred to another Commander's household in hopes that she will be able to repeat her success.

As Offred and the others return to their homes, each imagines carrying her own baby with her, and each feels her own failure. Offred addresses her absent mother, telling her to be thankful that there is now a "women's culture" (p. 159), although not the kind the feminists wanted.

Commentary

- Offred uses a kind of **irony** sometimes known as **understatement**. She carefully chooses words and phrases that imply criticism, without directly stating her condemnation of the Wives or the social system in general. For example, when she thinks of the Wives' buffet lunch, she uses the slang phrase "pig out" (p. 145). Later she describes them as they crowd around the newborn baby, some of them still carrying plates and wine glasses, some still chewing (p. 158). The picture is not pleasant, but Offred is not directly critical. In the same way, she implies criticism of the system that will now reassign Janine to another Commander's household, to "someone else who needs a turn" (p. 159). In this society, the Handmaids are objects to be used, shared or discarded by the ruling powers.

Chapter 22

Summary

Later in her room, Offred's exhausted mind reconstructs the story of what happened to Moira. Details passed from woman to woman at the Red Center were first told to Janine. Offred imagines a meeting when Aunt Lydia proposed that Janine become an informant. She told her about Moira's latest escape attempt, how she had lured Aunt Elizabeth into a washroom to help with a plugged toilet. Moira then used a long piece of metal from the toilet tank as a weapon to force Aunt Elizabeth to give up her whistle and cattle prod. In the basement furnace room, they exchanged clothes. Moira tied and gagged Aunt Elizabeth, and left her. Then, disguised and adopting a stern posture, Moira marched out of the Center, presented Aunt Elizabeth's pass to the Angels on guard and disappeared.

Aunt Lydia told Janine to keep her ears open – perhaps other Handmaids were part of Moira's plotting. Janine was happy to cooperate with Aunt Lydia; nevertheless, she passed the story on. The other Handmaids began avoiding her, knowing she was now a danger to them.

Meanwhile, Moira was out there somewhere, "a loose woman," possibly plotting the destruction of the Red Center. Moira appealed to the other Handmaids as a "fantasy" of rebellion (p. 167), making the Aunts seem somewhat absurd, their power flawed. They expected that Moira would be dragged back to face even worse punishment than she had on her previous escape attempt. But, says Offred, she has not yet reappeared.

Commentary

- While expanding the Janine subplot, Offred establishes a **second subplot**, centered on Moira. Offred has previously illustrated the attitude of her strong-willed friend about personal freedom. In her first escape attempt (Ch. 15), Moira demonstrated her determination to be independent while exploiting the system's weaknesses. Her second escape is a turning point. Moira disappeared from the Red Center, leaving the Handmaids to admire her audacity, although they themselves are beginning to feel secure in the Re-Education Center.

- For Offred, Janine and Moira represent opposing forces: conformity, security, loss of self on the one hand; and rebellion, risk, freedom of choice on the other.

CHAPTER 23

Summary

Offred thinks about the story she is telling, a reconstruction, a selection and arrangement of details in which she tries to find meaning. To prepare us for what comes next – her secret encounter with the Commander – she talks about forgiveness. Her story is about how she must eventually exert her own power by forgiving those who have control over her.

She sleeps briefly and is awakened by Cora with dinner, eager for news of Janine's baby. Like Offred, Cora wants to participate in Janine's success. Cora hopes they might soon have a baby in their own household and appeals to Offred to fulfill her obligation to the "team."

Offred suddenly remembers her appointment with the Commander. She goes quietly downstairs and along the corridor toward his office, knowing the meeting is illegal. As Handmaid, she is a breeder of children, not a courtesan for the Commander's personal pleasure. Punishment, imposed by Serena Joy who handles the "women's business," might be reclassification as an Unwoman. But Offred knows that to refuse the Commander, who holds real power, might cause worse trouble. The fact that he wants something intrigues her. She wonders how to take advantage of this weakness in him.

The Commander's office looks much like normal life in the time before: a desk with a computer, a potted plant, a pen-holder set and papers, a fireplace, a sofa and chairs. Most amazing to Offred, the shelves are lined with books in plain view, not locked secretly away.

The Commander greets her with an unconventional "Hello," placing a chair for her and seating himself behind the desk. He smiles reassuringly, in neither a sinister nor a predatory way. Offred feels a little like a child facing a parent. He comments that she must think this meeting strange, and says, "I want . . . ," but breaks off. Offred now understands this is to be a bargaining session and expects to take advantage of it. The Commander finally comes to the point. He wants to play a game of Scrabble. Offred almost shrieks with laughter. She remembers that Scrabble used to be a game for old folks in retirement homes and before that, for adolescents. Now it is a forbidden activity the Commander cannot enjoy with his Wife.

They play two games, and Offred enjoys recording the unusual words they create. The feel of the smooth letter tiles is voluptuous to her fingers, giving an unusual sense of freedom and luxury. She wins the first game and lets the Commander win the second.

Finally, he tells her it is time for her to go and listens for sounds in the darkened corridor. To Offred, their conspiracy has been like an old-fashioned date, when she would sneak into her college dormitory after hours. Then the Commander asks her to kiss him. Offred thinks about how she might do what Moira did at the Red Center: remove a sharp metal rod from the toilet tank to use as a weapon. She imagines killing him while pretending to offer her body.

Then she admits that this thought is only part of her "reconstruction" of the incident. At the time, no such thought occurs. Instead, she merely kisses him, mouth closed, without feeling. The Commander, embarrassed, says, "Not like that . . . . As if you meant it" (p. 176). Offred thinks, sympathetically, that he is "so sad."

Commentary

- One of the novel's central **themes** emerges in this episode: Who has real power and control in Offred's world? Three forms of power are evident. First, we know from preceding chapters that the Wives control the "women's business," everything to do with the household and the procreation of children. Second, Offred tells us the Commanders hold real power, although the political and military control she means is never directly illustrated. A third kind of power, bargaining power, resides in Offred herself, as she finds she can choose to give or withhold favors.

- For the first time in the novel we see Commander Fred up close. This shadowy representative of the government's patriarchal authority becomes human. The formality of his role as Commander is gone, as Offred describes his awkward and "sheepish" behavior. She compares him to a schoolboy in the time before, trying to please his first date. His demands are clear enough, but seem juvenile – games of Scrabble, a kiss "as if you meant it." She also sees the human side of the man who had previously been only a symbol of authority and feels a need to forgive him as an individual.

Opposing influences

Offred's internal struggle is between the limitations of forced conformity and the possibilities of rebellion (see Chapter 13). As a Handmaid, she is influenced in her thinking and behavior by Janine the conformist and Moira the rebel.

```
                    ┌──────────────┐
                  ↗ │    OFFRED    │ ↖
                    └──────────────┘
```

JANINE conforms: society controls her whole life	**MOIRA rebels: she finds the system's weaknesses**
• through the rigid Aunts	• to exploit subversive flaws
• through brain-washing methods	• to fulfill individual needs
• through public humiliation	• to maintain personal freedoms
• through religious precepts	• to assert her independence
• through severe military rule	• to protect her sense of self

PART IX • NIGHT • Chapter 24

Summary

Back in her room, Offred ponders her encounter with the Commander and her changing sense of herself. Then she decides she can live only in the present, and to do so she must take stock of her situation. There is no going back to the life before. She is 33 years old, 5-foot, 7-inches tall and has "viable ovaries." This is her last chance to fulfill her role as Handmaid.

But as of tonight, the situation has changed. She can bargain with the Commander.

She recalls the implicit truth behind Aunt Lydia's instructions about men, that they want just one thing and can be manipulated. Offred finds it hard to see the Commander in this way, with his desire for Scrabble games and his need to be kissed. She finds the situation bizarre, but she recognizes the seriousness of her own position.

She recalls a television documentary about Nazi Germany that she saw as a child of seven. Many years after the events of World War II, a woman, the former mistress of a cruel and brutal Nazi leader, was still practicing "how not to think." She had sympathized with her lover, had truly believed he was no monster. In this way, she could go on living, believing in ordinary human decency. Then, just a few days after the filmed interview, the aging woman had killed herself.

Offred feels that something in her is about to erupt. She tries to suppress wild laughter, knowing that such hysteria would attract attention and mean disaster for her. On her knees, holding in the laughter, she crawls into the cupboard, stifling the sounds in the folds of her hanging cloak.

The fit passes. In the darkness, she touches the Latin inscription left by the other Handmaid: *Nolite te bastardes carborundorum*. It seems now not so much a prayer, but more like a command, yet she still has no idea of its meaning. She lies on the floor, gradually relaxing, listening to her own heartbeat.

Commentary

- Offred's sense of herself, of her place in the social framework, is changing. She is learning about personal power, the control she may be able to use. "Context is all," she tells us (p. 180). She means that within the specific situation of the Commander's study she is once again a person, not just a breeder in society's program for repopulation.

- The digression about the Nazi mistress suggests – with Atwood's typical understatement – Offred's understanding of her new arrangement with the Commander. She implies that her situation is parallel with that of the Nazi mistress. Offred is finding it easy "to invent a humanity" for the Commander, the representative of oppressive authority.

PART X • SOUL SCROLLS • Chapter 25

Summary

Offred is awakened by Cora, who drops the breakfast tray when she finds the Handmaid asleep in the closet. Cora slyly suggests a small conspiracy, to cover for the wasted eggs by pretending that Offred has eaten them. There will be less trouble if Rita does not have to cook another breakfast.

In the garden, Offred sees Serena Joy snipping seed pods with her garden shears. Offred amuses herself thinking of romantic gardens in old-fashioned poetry. Her sensual nature, musing about suggestive words like "swoon" and "rendezvous," seems dangerous in the warm weather. She mentions briefly how she almost flirted with a checkpoint Guardian by letting him catch a glimpse of her ankle.

She explains the new "arrangement," how Nick, the chauffeur, signals her by wearing his hat crooked on those days when she is to visit the Commander after dinner. Such meetings can happen only when Serena Joy is out, perhaps visiting a sick Wife. The Wives get sick a lot, while Handmaids and Marthas avoid being sick – or being seen to be sick – if possible. Lingering illness, weakness of any kind, would be "terminal" for a Handmaid.

Her first meeting with the Commander had been something of a letdown. Offred had almost expected some perverse sexual activity, fulfillment of his illegal desires. Scrabble games seemed a joke. She wondered what the bargaining terms between them could be.

Their second meeting begins in the same way, but after two games of Scrabble, the Commander offers a present – an old magazine with glossy images of lovely models in makeup and fashionable clothes. Such magazines offered the promise of a life of ever-changing adventures stretching out into the future. The Commander assures her that here in his study, where they have already broken more serious taboos, the magazine is a minor offense. Offred eagerly devours the pictures, imagining the models' free and independent lives. According to the Aunts' rules she should feel evil, but instead she feels "naughty."

The Commander explains that those of his rank, who are beyond reproach, can safely amuse themselves with such "dangerous" magazines. And it pleases him to share it with her. Besides, he says, he no longer has much in common with Serena Joy. Offred is amused, thinking of the old cliché of adulterers: "His wife didn't understand him" (p. 197).

At their third meeting, Offred asks the Commander for hand lotion and explains about using butter or margarine. He warns her not to use the lotion at times when she will be close to Serena Joy. On the fourth night, he gives her some unlabelled lotion that smells faintly of vegetable oil. When Offred tells him she cannot keep it in her room, the Commander appears truly ignorant of the Handmaids' living conditions – the close scrutiny they endure, the suspicions they might have black market items like books or razor blades, the implication they might be contemplating suicide. Offred loses her temper as she tells him this. "You ought to know," she says, but the Commander does not react. He merely suggests she keep the lotion in his study.

As Offred applies the lotion to her hands and face, she feels a little embarrassed at the way he watches her. She feels that, for him, she is only an amusement.

Commentary

- This chapter provides further insights into **character**. Commander Fred has poise, dignity and reserve as a representative of institutional and domestic power. But in the study, he ignores the rules and amuses himself with Offred's companionship. He becomes sensitive to her concerns and accepts criticism.

- Offred reveals her romantic nature in the spring weather. She recalls sensual, dangerous words associated with freedom of thought and feeling. In the study, she becomes more assertive, expressing some independence of thought. Her feeling that she has some bargaining power allows her to criticize the Commander. Nevertheless, she remains self-conscious about how he watches her. Although she might like to be considered important to him, she must remember she is merely a "whim."

Chapter 26

Summary

When the night of the Ceremony comes around again, Offred is aware of how her relationship with the Commander has changed. Instead of feeling detached, she now feels shy and uncomfortable. The Commander is no longer a one-dimensional figure, because their intimacy, whatever its significance, has made their relationship more complicated.

Her feelings about Serena Joy have changed also. Her former hatred of the Wife is now mixed with jealousy and guilt. Offred wonders why she cares, since Serena Joy surely has no feelings for her and would quickly be rid of Offred if she had any excuse. Still, Offred enjoys having a certain advantage over Serena Joy.

The Commander almost gives her away though, by tentatively reaching up to touch her face. Offred successfully puts him off. When they are alone together again in his study, she reminds him that he could easily get her exiled to the Colonies. The Commander complains that he finds the mating ritual "impersonal," and Offred mocks him for taking so long to realize that.

Offred recalls one of Aunt Lydia's pronouncements, about how much better things will be for future generations. Women will enjoy bonds of affection, all working toward one end. Population will grow, and Handmaids will not have to be transferred from family to family. Meanwhile, they must not be too greedy. Offred concludes that she is, for now, the Commander's mistress, providing what is missing in his married life even if it is only secret Scrabble games.

Sometimes Offred thinks there must be collusion between the Commander and Serena Joy, that the Wife is secretly laughing at her, just as Offred sometimes laughs with ironic self-knowledge at herself. Nevertheless, she feels happier than she had been. The Commander is now of greater interest to her, as she is more interesting to him. She knows she is no longer just an empty, waiting womb.

Commentary

* Offred demonstrates ironic self-awareness in describing her advantage over Serena Joy. By mocking the Commander, she displays the new found power she now has in criticizing the system, and she shows an intelligent awareness of the kind of nonsense on which Gilead society is based. She may not be able to escape strict controls and rituals imposed on her, but she can ridicule the Commander's unthinking allegiance to their foolishness.

Chapter 27

Summary

On a warm summer day, Offred and Ofglen are returning from shopping. Offred describes the easier relationship they now have. They no longer bother with formal greetings, but simply move off on their way, sometimes varying the route while keeping within the barriers that mark their area of the city: "A rat in a maze is free to go anywhere," says Offred, "as long as it stays inside the maze" (p. 206).

They pause briefly at the Wall, but there are no bodies today. When there are bodies, Offred is reassured that she does not recognize Luke, and she can then go on believing he is still alive. Somehow she is sure Luke is a prisoner in one of the university buildings that now belong to the secret police.

Offred and Ofglen continue on their way to a franchise outlet called "Soul Scrolls," where computerized printers produce endless rolls of prayers. These are ordered (and paid for, making "a lot of profit") through phone contacts by faithful and pious believers, such as the Wives. Inside the unmanned shop, visitors can listen to the machine-like voices of the printers repeating prayers over and over.

Watching the machines through the glass, Offred is suddenly aware that she is looking into the reflection of Ofglen's eyes. She is aware of the risk in this close contact, even though they are alone. Ofglen breaks the silence by whispering, wondering whether God listens to the machines' prayers. Offred recognizes her question as treason – "subversion, sedition, blasphemy, heresy all rolled into one" (p. 210). But she answers "No" and sees Ofglen let out her breath in relief.

Ofglen reassures Offred that it is safe to talk in whispers, here in the open where they seem to be praying. As they walk on, Ofglen indicates that there is an underground resistance movement. Offred wants to ask her friend whether she knows anything about Moira, Luke, her daughter and her mother, but they are now too close to the manned barriers.

In the warm sun, there are more people on the street than usual. Suddenly, there is a commotion as a black van cruises by. Offred, afraid that they have been detected in their treasonous talk, tries to ignore what is happening. Two Eyes leap from the van, grab an ordinary-looking pedestrian and throw him into the back of the vehicle. The incident is over in seconds. Offred is relieved: "It wasn't me."

Commentary

- We are reminded again of forbidden activities under the repressive totalitarian regime in Gilead. For example, the ban on reading has led to extensive use of visual symbols, "sign language," as Offred half-mockingly says. Face-to-face contact between the Handmaids is a risk, and their whispered conversation must be covered with a pretense of pious interest in the computerized prayers. To emphasize the dangers Offred and Ofglen manage to avoid, we are given a brief glimpse of the secret police at work. Note that this incident is placed at the end of a chapter that began with Offred's comments about the Wall, where executed criminals are routinely displayed.

- The "Soul Scrolls" idea is a very old one, common in several religious traditions. Offred herself mentions "Tibetan prayer wheels" (p. 210), devices that were turned continuously by wind or water to deliver unending petitions in Tibetan Buddhism. In Gilead, the non-stop prayers are produced on computer printouts (constantly recycling the paper) after payment is charged to the purchaser's computer account.

- The **main plot** moves forward in this chapter. For the first time,

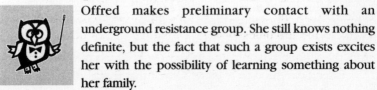 Offred makes preliminary contact with an underground resistance group. She still knows nothing definite, but the fact that such a group exists excites her with the possibility of learning something about her family.

Chapter 28

Summary

Later the same day, Offred sits at her window, remembering her friend Moira's attitude regarding Offred's illicit affair with Luke. Offred was "poaching" on another woman's territory, said Moira, but Offred had insisted that Luke made his own decisions. This was shortly after Moira had revealed she was a lesbian, and Offred in return accused her friend of having no scruples in "borrowing" other women. The argument had continued, but ended in laughing and hugging.

In the past, Offred worked in a small library, but the idea of women having jobs, of everyday things like paper money, now seems ancient to her. The computerized banking system assisted the revolutionary coup that established the Republic of Gilead. After the assassination of the president and much of the U.S. Congress, the army declared a state of emergency and suspended the Constitution. The stunned populace waited, wondering who the unseen enemy really were. Moira warned Offred that a big change was coming, especially for educated and independent women like themselves. Newspapers were censored, some eliminated. Roadblocks appeared, and "Identipasses" were required for security reasons. The pornography industry was shut down. The new regime said elections would be held, but would take some time to prepare. Meanwhile, life was to go on as usual.

Some time later, when Offred and Luke were married and their daughter was about four years old, another major change occurred. Offred found that her Compunumber was no longer valid for purchases. At the library, the frightened director informed Offred and the other women that they could no longer hold jobs. Armed men in uniforms stood ready to enforce this new law.

Moira at that time worked in the publishing division of a women's organization. She was able to fill in a few more details. For example, every Compucard marked with an "F" for female was now invalid, the bank account frozen. Women could no longer hold property, although their male relatives could access the accounts.

Later, Luke tried to reassure Offred that it was probably just a temporary situation. But Offred remembered noticing that the armed enforcers at the library had not been regular military men. Their uniforms were of some other army.

Protest marches followed, mostly by women, but they were smaller than expected because of fear among ordinary citizens. When the new police began to open fire on the marchers, the protests stopped. Examination of private computer records and door-to-door searches began. Offred stayed at home, thinking about her family and tearfully worrying about their future.

She recalls an earlier time, when she was about fourteen years old. Her mother had brought home a group of her female friends after one of their women's movement marches. They dressed in unfeminine overalls, talked too loudly and swore too much. Offred disapproved of her mother's activities then, but now she wishes her mother were here.

Offred sees Nick below her window. She admires his muscular body and remembers how they held each other in the sitting room before her first private meeting with the Commander. Nick is now wearing his cap sideways, the usual signal from the Commander. Offred wonders what the chauffeur gets out of the arrangement, what he has bargained for in keeping the Commander's activities secret.

Offred's thoughts return again to Luke, to the night when she lost her job. She felt a change in their relationship. They were no longer "each other's" she says; instead, she was his, and he did not seem to mind the change. She could not ask him about it then, because she was so afraid of losing him.

Commentary

- Some of the **historical background** regarding the coup that established the Republic of Gilead is filled in from the point of view of ordinary citizens, Offred, Moira and Luke. It was a time of growing fear and of restrictions on freedom of choice, especially for women. So began the subservient role for females, demonstrated in the Handmaids' "re-education" and in Offred's present situation.

- This chapter provides additional comment on Offred's changing relationships with men. The "Moira" side of her own nature might disapprove of her activities with the Commander, but she has already told us that she is happier now in the household than she had been. The brief contact she had with Nick is on her mind. Her renewed sense of her "self" has reawakened the sexual side of her nature. She can admit now her doubts about Luke's change of attitude in the time before their attempted escape from Gilead.

- The feminist/anti-feminist **theme** is highlighted in this chapter. Female independence was suppressed at the time of the Gilead coup, and women were subjected to the control of their male relatives. Atwood satirizes reaction to the women's movement of the 1970s, and the religious laws enforced under Muslim fundamentalist leaders in Iran in the 1980s. Even more restrictive controls on women were implemented under the Taliban regime in Afghanistan in the 1990s.

Chapter 29

Summary

The same evening in the Commander's office, Offred tries to draw him out about himself. He tells her a few facts, without going into details – "market research . . . a sort of scientist." Then Offred takes a chance, unable to stop herself from heading into danger. Without stating the source, she asks about the Latin phrase, *Nolite te bastardes carborundorum*. The Commander laughs as he tells her about childhood Latin jokes. He takes an old textbook from a shelf, and shows her more examples. On one page, the same phrase, written with a child's pen, appears beside a picture of a famous statue doctored with scrawled graffiti. He explains the meaning, "Don't let the bastards grind you down," grinning like a freckled schoolboy himself. Offred says she almost likes him at this moment.

Then she realizes that the Handmaid who scratched the message probably saw it here, in the Commander's study. Offred bluntly asks what happened to her. "She hanged herself," says the

Commander. "Serena found out." That was why the hook and light fixture were removed in Offred's room.

Offred suggests that it might be better if they did not meet secretly again, but he protests that he wants their sessions to continue. She realizes that now she has a real bargaining strength, "something on him" – his need to justify his role in the system by helping her and his feeling of guilt for the other Handmaid's suicide. If he can make life "bearable" for Offred, then what he and the others in power are doing would seem right after all.

She bargains with him, this time for more than hand lotion. She wants to know, she says, "whatever there is to know." She wants to know, "What's going on?"

Commentary

- The Commander's frank revelation about the Handmaid who committed suicide gives Offred a further advantage in their relationship. By accepting favors and gifts, she is doing him a favor – helping him rationalize the authoritarian power he and the others hold over the lives of ordinary people like her. Offred's intelligent grasp of this situation gives her the confidence to ask for firsthand information, but her simple question seems almost comically innocent. Nevertheless, it sums up the years of fear and confusion she has suffered through, something she has no doubt wanted to ask during all that time: "What's going on?"

Features of totalitarianism

In real life and in dystopian fiction, most totalitarian societies incorporate certain common features intended to establish and maintain centralized power and control over the general population. Examples are readily found in The Handmaid's Tale.

Totalitarian Society	The Handmaid's Tale
• Right-wing forces infiltrate the established government, take power by force if necessary and begin the revolutionary movement to stabilize the new regime's control.	• President's Day Massacre: the U.S. President and many in Congress assassinated; the Constitution suspended.
• Strict enforcement of martial law suppresses all dissent.	• Military forces, including a new "army" of Guardians.
• Authorities restrict freedom of movement.	• Offred and Luke attempt escape.
• Leaders take control of resources and the economy – all personal financial activity, including the purchase of goods and services.	• Compucard transactions cut off for females; available goods and food restricted.
• Secret police and domestic spy networks operate throughout the social structure.	• Eyes enforce domestic security; neighbor spies on neighbor.
• Special forces identify and persecute non-conformist groups.	• Catholics, Baptists, Quakers, Jews identified as enemies.
• Identifiable minority groups are interned in forced labor camps.	• African-Americans resettled in Homeland farming areas.
• Propaganda – manipulation of the media – becomes the only source of information.	• Limited TV news; outside signals blocked; reading forbidden.
• Mass demonstrations support the regime. The general population must participate in ceremonies, displays, criminal trials, executions.	• Pravaganzas, Salvagings, Particicution ceremonies.
• Centralized authority claims jurisdiction overall aspects of society on traditional political and/or religious principles.	• Republic of Gilead claims biblical authority and precedent of "traditional" values.

PART XI • NIGHT • Chapter 30

Summary

At her window, Offred watches the night, lit by moon and searchlight, scented with summer flowers. She sees Nick cross the lawn. She is too frightened of her own feelings to admit that she hungers for his touch.

Somehow her mind and body can keep memories of Luke separate from her present longings. She recalls the night before their attempted escape. Luke pointed out that something must be done about their cat, but that he would take care of "it." Nevertheless, their careful planning was useless. The authorities had been waiting for them at the border. Offred now finds it difficult to remember what Luke and her daughter even looked like.

She decides to pray, and her prayer is simple. She would like to know what God is up to and prays that whatever it is, He will help her get through it. She prays that the others are safe – Luke, her daughter, her mother, Moira. She prays to be free of temptation. Temptation for Offred is wanting to know, and she thinks now that maybe she could not bear to know more than she does. She thinks too much about suicide – the other Handmaid's use of the chandelier and the possibility of using a hook in the closet. Finally she decides she must continue to live, "In Hope," the phrase often inscribed on gravestones.

She feels very alone, and although she manages a small joke about that, quoting an old song, "All alone by the telephone," she wonders how she can keep on living.

Commentary

• Offred faces several unpleasant truths about herself. First, in the incident regarding the cat, she recognizes her own weakness. By not taking some part in the responsibility for killing the pet, she had "killed" some part of her own humanity. Second, she recognizes her continuing fears about her family. Finally, at the end of her unconventional version of the Lord's Prayer, she seems not strengthened, but close to despair. To die "In Hope," is still to die. In the structure of the novel, this particular "Night" interlude marks a turning point. Offred's growing self-awareness, despite her cry of despair, is a stronger note in her character.

PART XII • JEZEBEL'S • Chapter 31

Summary
On a day in July, Offred and Ofglen walk as usual to the Wall. Two bodies are hanging there. From the symbols attached to them, Offred knows one is a Catholic, though not a priest. The other is marked with a "J" she is not sure about – not a Jew, whose symbol would be a yellow star – possibly a Jehovah's Witness or Jesuit.

They head for an open space where they will be able to carry on a whispered conversation, across a small park area near a building that used to be Memorial Hall. Ofglen remarks that the building is now where the Eyes hold their banquets, and says she knows this from the underground grapevine. She explains to Offred about the password, "Mayday," used by members of the network. She reminds Offred how she had once tried it on her. Offred had recognized only the French origin of the old distress call: "*M'aidez* – Help me" (Ch. 8).

Offred returns home, passing Serena Joy in her garden. Her mistress invites the Handmaid to sit. She inquires indirectly if there has been any sign of pregnancy in Offred. Offred answers no. Serena Joy offers scant sympathy, noting that the Handmaid's time is running out. She then suggests that perhaps the Commander is unable to father a child. This startles Offred, and for the first time since their initial meeting, they look directly at each other.

Serena Joy suggests that Offred might try another way to become pregnant, and when Offred protests about the danger, the Wife simply says that unofficially it is often done. Offred wonders if it might be by a doctor, remembering her experience with the doctor who offered to "help" her (Ch. 11). Serena Joy explains that that was how Ofwarren – Janine – became pregnant, and that it was done with the Wife's knowledge. She offers to make sure that nothing would go wrong, but Offred declines. Serena Joy agrees because doctors sometimes try to blackmail those involved. Instead she suggests someone they can trust: Nick, who has been with them a long time.

Offred realizes that Nick probably runs black-market errands, getting Serena Joy's cigarettes for example, and that this might be his usual reward. When Offred wonders about the Commander's part in such a scheme, Serena Joy is firm: "We just won't tell him." Offred repeats her concern about the risk involved, but they both know she is at risk even if they do not try this. She may soon be sent away as an Unwoman.

She agrees to Serena Joy's plan. Immediately the Wife offers something Offred wants in return: she will bring a picture of her daughter. Offred chokes back her anger that Serena Joy has probably known all along where the child is and has refused to give her any comforting news. But Offred knows she must not reveal her anger, not when there is hope. As they part, Serena Joy, smiling about their shared secrets, puts a cigarette in her hand and tells her to get a match from Rita.

Commentary

- More details emerge about the methods of the totalitarian society in executing religious criminals. The use of yellow stars to identify Jewish victims is a direct reference to Nazi practice in the death camps of World War II.
- The use of "Mayday" as the underground's password is a clever touch of **symbolism**, indicated in Offred's understanding of the word's original meaning. That the underground can "help me" feeds Offred's hope, signalling rejection of the near-despair she experienced in the previous chapter.
- Serena Joy, like the Commander, typifies the corruption that exists even among high-ranking authorities. Her sharing of secret plans and rewards demonstrates how far she is willing to risk exposure – and Offred's life – to improve her own status among the Wives.

Chapter 32

Summary

After getting a match from Rita, Offred hurries to her room, eagerly anticipating a rush of nicotine from the cigarette. Then she imagines another possibility: using the match to burn the house down and escape.

She thinks about meetings with the Commander. Sometimes, she says, they become childish as they play Scrabble, cheating and giggling over made-up words. Occasionally he turns on his short-wave radio, to Radio Free America, but only briefly, to show her that he can get away with what is forbidden. Sometimes he amuses himself by pretending to be subservient to her. Offred finds it hard to reconcile this with Ofglen's comment that the Commander is at the top of the regime's power structure.

Offred tries to understand their relationship by seeing herself from his position. She knows why he wants to please her: in return for gifts and favors, he wants true intimacy. Sometimes he becomes argumentative, trying to explain the background of the revolution. He says the real problem was not with women achieving their own kinds of independence. The problem was in leaving men with no role as protectors. They were being denied emotional involvement, even in marriage. Men like himself still need emotional intimacy, but Offred is not prepared to give that.

He wants to know what she thinks, her opinion about what the political and military powers have done. Offred holds back, afraid to express her inner self. She claims she has no opinion, but he knows what she really thinks and tries to justify what they have done. "You can't make an omelette without breaking eggs," he says. "We thought we could do better" (p. 264). Offred wonders how they can consider this present situation "better," and the Commander replies, "Better never means better for everyone. . . . It always means worse for some."

Commentary

- The Commander's short-wave radio is a reference to Radio Free Europe during World War II. Broadcasts originating outside German-occupied countries subverted Nazi propaganda, keeping the victims of Nazi aggression informed of the Allied war effort.

- The Commander's justification for the revolution is weak, although the thinking behind it is real enough. As a writer of speculative fiction, Atwood takes social problems to extremes in order to teach and warn. Religious and political reaction against the women's movement becomes a violent military overthrow of democratic freedoms, where women are the principal victims.

Chapter 33

Summary
On a summer afternoon, Offred and Ofglen, matched by other pairs of Handmaids, attend a Women's Prayvaganza. They pass armed Guardians outside a banner-draped university building and move into a closed courtyard. On one side, wooden chairs are filling up with Wives and children of high-ranking officials. Galleries contain the lower-class women, Marthas and Econowives. The Handmaids kneel in rows within a roped-off area. Ofglen leads Offred toward the back, where they will be able to talk, and Offred notes the whispering all around her.

Ofglen draws her attention to Janine and reveals that her baby, Angela, was a "shredder" after all, and Janine's second failure as a Handmaid. Ofglen says a doctor was the father. Now Janine believes her failure was a punishment for sin. Offred guesses that Ofglen gets such information by eavesdropping on the Wives' gossiping, and wonders if Serena Joy will gossip about the plan involving Nick.

Offred recalls a morning at the Red Center, a time before Moira's second escape attempt, when Janine had a breakdown. She seemed demented, smiling fixedly, repeating sentences from her past when she once worked in a restaurant. Moira brought her back, slapping her and warning that if she went "too far away" like that, the Aunts would take her upstairs to the Chemistry Lab and shoot her, afterward burning her remains like garbage. Moira warned the others: "You can't let her go slipping over the edge. . . . That stuff is catching" (p. 272).

Commentary

- The Prayvaganza reveals another feature of this totalitarian society, the involvement of all classes in the religious underpinnings of Gilead. The entertainment value of the show encourages mass participation.

- In this and the following chapter, Atwood satirizes revival meetings, mass demonstrations of a community's devotion to accepted religious principles. Multiple weddings are performed at such mass meetings in some religious cults.

- The Janine **subplot** develops in two time frames. In the present, we see Janine blaming herself for failure following her Birth Day success. She now embodies the suffering that all Handmaids face as child-bearers. In the past, Janine's breakdown reveals a shaky hold on reality, an outcome of her tendency toward self-abasement in the Testifying episode of Chapter 13.

Chapter 34

Summary

The Prayvaganza continues with the mass marriage of twenty newly decorated Angels to twenty veiled daughters given away by the Wives. Offred wonders whether these girls, some as young as fourteen, remember anything about the time before. After two generations, such daughters will never have known anything but their silent lives, dressed in white, obedient to authority.

Offred recalls a conversation with her Commander about the past. He reminded her of how females used to suffer, as single women, as abused wives, as working mothers. Now they have full support to "fulfill their biological destinies." According to Offred, the authorities ignored love. The Commander dismissed that idea, insisting arranged marriages always worked out just as well as, or better than, falling in love. Those years of romantic love were a fluke in history, but now society has returned "to Nature's norm."

Conducting the group wedding, a Commander reads from the Bible, an epistle of St. Paul on the duties of women: "subjection . . .

silence . . . faith and charity and holiness with sobriety" (I Timothy, 2: 9-15). Ofglen, whispering, sarcastically comments that the Wives should be warned about "sobriety" when they are into their sherry.

Offred watches as the veils of the girls are lifted for the exchange of rings. The Angels may also qualify for Handmaids, especially if their new Wives do not produce children. But the girls, thinks Offred, are stuck with these husbands, "zits and all." Do not worry about love, she says sarcastically. Just "do your duty in silence . . . flat on your back."

Offred again recalls Aunt Lydia, talking about women all working together to make the system work. Moira had been contemptuous and liked to imagine obscene activities among those in power. Offred objected to Moira's lewd ideas, but she knows now that imagining and whispering obscenities is itself a powerful way to subvert authority. She now pictures obscene and failing sex scenes involving the "drained white brides" and their new husbands.

As they are leaving, Ofglen tells Offred that they in the Mayday group know she is seeing her Commander alone. Ofglen wonders what he really wants, and Offred finds that hard to explain. Ofglen urges her to find out any inside information she can from the Commander.

Commentary

- The Prayvaganza ceremony with its mass marriage illustrates again the conformity imposed on women in the Republic of Gilead. Offred's sarcastic thoughts provide the author's point of view on the subject and undermine the Commander's government-approved ideas about love and marriage.
- From the chapter's final incident, we learn that Ofglen and the underground movement with which she is in contact have sources of information that Offred knows nothing about. How have they learned about her secret meetings with the Commander?
- Offred's character has changed considerably by this point in the novel. She is more aware, more curious, more critical of society.

Chapter 35

Summary

In her room, Offred starts to recall the escape attempt with Luke, but that story is too painful. Instead she will just withdraw into herself. *Nolite te bastardes carborundorum* did the other Handmaid no good, so why try to fight? Then she scolds herself for thinking this way.

Again she recalls the Commander's sneering comments about falling in love. Offred believes love is central to understanding oneself, and anyone who misses it is somehow non-human. Her thoughts wander through wordplay about "falling" and "fallen women." Then she recalls the religious injunction, "God is love," and says they used to reverse that: "Love is God." She thinks about being in love and feels comfort in remembering those times with Luke. Then she thinks about "working out" to keep your body in shape for a man, so that the love between you might "work out," or you might "work out" your problems together. Offred finds it strange how they used to think they had complete freedom to shape their own lives.

She finds herself crying. She says she is a "refugee from the past," going over what she has been forced to leave behind. Now she can only wait for whatever comes next.

There is a knock at her door, but instead of Cora with her dinner tray, Serena Joy enters. She offers a photograph but warns that she must return it before it is missed. Offred looks at the image, wondering if this is indeed her daughter. The girl is tall, smiling. Offred cannot bear the thought that she has been obliterated from the girl's fading memory.

Later, as she eats her dinner, she notes how she is provided with only a fork and a spoon. They cut up her meat for her and never provide her with a knife.

Commentary

- Once again Offred demonstrates an interest in **wordplay**. In a society where the simple act of reading words is a crime, such wordplay, like the Scrabble games with the Commander, is another kind of subversive rebellion. Many more examples of Offred's – and Atwood's – fondness for wordplay can be found in the novel.

- In earlier chapters, Offred has suggested several times the hidden potential for violence in society. Suicide and acts of vengeance directed at authorities are often on her mind. She has herself told us of wanting to obtain a weapon – Serena Joy's garden shears, for example. At the end of this chapter, she is thinking about how her child was taken from her to be raised as someone else's daughter. She gives her strongest indication yet of the intensity and persistence of the hatred and anger she feels. As usual, she does it indirectly, by commenting on the cutlery provided with dinner: fork and spoon, but never a knife.

Chapter 36

Summary

When Offred enters the Commander's study, he says he has a "little surprise" for her and offers a costume trimmed with mauve and pink feathers, and purple sequins. Offred knows that all such clothing was supposed to have been destroyed. She speaks disapprovingly about wearing the garment but still admits being attracted to the idea of dressing up. The Commander explains that it is a disguise. She will need to wear makeup as well, to fit in at the nightclub where he plans to take her. She understands the risk, especially to herself, but wants a break in the respectable routine of her life.

While the Commander turns his back, Offred modestly puts on the ill-fitting costume. As makeup, the Commander can supply only lipstick, eyeliner and mascara. Offred, out of practice, finally puts on the makeup, using a hand mirror she recognizes as Serena Joy's. The Commander is pleased and excited, as if they were going to a party. He brings out a cloak and hood, blue in color. Offred thinks it is probably Serena Joy's also.

Nick drives them through the dark streets. From his straight and rigid posture, Offred imagines he disapproves of her tonight. She wonders if he obtained the costume she is wearing under her Wife disguise. She almost wants him to feel "angry or lustful or envious."

When they reach their destination, the Commander's instructions to Nick about when to return suggest that he has done this before.

Offred catches Nick's eye watching her as she leaves the car. Again she wonders how he feels toward her. She worries about her ridiculous appearance and imagines Moira playfully calling her an idiot.

Commentary

- Offred's growing concern about Nick's feelings reflects her new interest in the chauffeur as another kind of risk she is prepared to take. Serena Joy has suggested Nick as a sexual partner, and Offred finds herself wanting to understand him.
- The brief mention of Moira, as Offred's unofficial conscience, inner guide or mocking voice of reason, prepares us for their reunion in the following chapters.
- The hypocrisy of the Commander is clear: he is betraying his wife, the Gilead ideals and his own beliefs in their outing.

Chapter 37

Summary

The Commander leads Offred into a carpeted hallway with soft lighting and numbered doors. In a central courtyard, several stories high with a skylight above, there is a fountain, and glass-walled elevators moving up and down. Offred recognizes this as a hotel, one of the places where she and Luke met secretly before his divorce.

Offred stares about her at the lounging and strolling women, and the men mingling with them. The men wear nondescript business suits or uniforms, but the women are "tropical" in the color and variety of their glittering costumes. The effect is of a masquerade party, big children dressed up to enjoy themselves. But Offred wonders whether there is any real joy here, whether these women have chosen to be here. She suspects it is an elegant brothel.

The Commander warns her not to stare, to act natural. He speaks to a male acquaintance, explaining only that Offred is new, holding her arm and almost imperceptibly straightening his pose. He becomes more youthful, as if he is showing her off and at the same time showing off to her – a little pathetic, she thinks, but understandable.

They sit for a while, and the Commander asks how she likes this "little club" for officers, senior officials and trade delegations. Although such activities may be forbidden, men need variety as part of the "procreational strategy." Women used to provide the variety by wearing many different outfits. With irony that the Commander does not recognize, Offred says, "So now that we don't have different clothes, you merely have different women" (p. 298). His reply annoys her. "It solves a lot of problems," he says. He explains that some of the women are prostitutes, and some are former professional women who prefer this life to the alternatives.

When he leaves to get her a drink, Offred sees her old friend Moira, talking with other women by the fountain. Moira is dressed absurdly in an ill-fitting, strapless outfit with a puff of white tail attached at the back, fake rabbit ears on her head, black net stockings, high heels. The whole costume reminds Offred of something from the past that she cannot quite place.

Moira notices Offred, but does not immediately react. They stare at each other, keeping their faces blank. Then Moira motions slightly with her head – the old signal about meeting in the washroom. When the Commander returns with the drinks, Offred asks directions. Unsteady in her high heels, she walks off-balance across the room.

Commentary

- The colorful scene at "Jezebel's" provides a sharp **contrast** to the Prayvaganza in Chapters 33 and 34 and illustrates the hypocrisy

undermining society. The **ideal** that God-fearing Gilead represents is in conflict with the **reality** of pleasure-seeking self-interest.

• The Commander reveals more of the youthful side of his character. Although it may be a "pathetic" display, Offred finds him almost likeable.

- Moira's reappearance adds a touch of humor in this dark novel. Margaret Atwood's ironic enjoyment of the feminism debate is reflected in Moira's outfit. Her costume is that of a "Playboy Bunny," a "hostess" in the private clubs established by Hugh Hefner's *Playboy Magazine* organization in the 1960s. Ironically, these clubs were a prime target of the women's movement.

Chapter 38

Summary

In the washroom, Moira assures the other women that she knows Offred; only then can the old friends hug. Offred explains that her Commander has smuggled her in just for tonight. Moira is, as usual, contemptuous of the Commanders: seeing a Handmaid all painted up is "just another crummy power trip," she says. Offred considers this, but feels that it is too simple as an explanation for Commander Fred's motivation.

Moira explains what happened after her escape from the Red Center. In her Aunt disguise, she expected to just keep going, with no clear plan. She assumed the authorities had arrested all of the women's publishing group she had worked for, and she knew they would soon be on the lookout for a fake Aunt on foot. From the printing group's old mailing list, Moira recalled a Quaker couple that might help her. She entered their house without trouble and then revealed who she was. The couple gave her a change of clothes and then escorted her to another Quaker house that was a station on the Underground Femaleroad (p. 310). The underground collaborators were well organized and had even infiltrated some useful places. A post office driver took Moira into the main part of the city in a mail sack.

Moira says the experience all sounds easy, but it was not. She was terrified at the time, and was certainly aware that others were risking their own lives in trying to save hers. She remained underground eight or nine months and managed to get as far north as Maine. The plan was to smuggle her to Canada by boat, but she and the helpers at that stage were captured.

Facing torture, Moira thought of suicide but was too well guarded. She refuses to talk about what was done to her: "They didn't leave any marks," she says (p. 312). They showed her a movie about life in the Colonies, where Unwomen and others spend their time cleaning up – cremating the bodies of military casualties and decontaminating toxic dumps and radiation spills. The workers have about three years before the contamination kills them. They are mostly old women, failed Handmaids, and incorrigibles like herself – "discards, all of us," Moira says. They are sterilized surgically if they are not already sterile. There are also men, she says; not all of the Gender Traitors end up on the Wall. They wear gray dresses, women and men.

They told her she had a choice: the Colonies or working in a brothel. Moira says she is no martyr and chose the sterility operation and Jezebel's. She suggests that Offred should figure out some way of getting herself here, but the suggestion frightens Offred. She thinks that they have taken away something important in Moira, and wants her friend to continue to display what she herself lacks – risk-taking, courage, independence. Moira understands Offred's thinking, and teases her, explaining that she will be all right. The Aunts assume the women at Jezebel's are all damned anyway and have given up trying to save them. The Commanders do not care what they do in their off time and are even entertained or excited by the idea of women who are sexually active among themselves.

Offred says to the reader that she would like to tell Moira's story another way, how her friend escaped for good, or blew up Jezebel's while fifty Commanders were inside. She would like to say that Moira's story ended in some spectacular, heroic manner, but she does not know how Moira's story ended. She never saw her again.

Commentary

- This chapter completes the subplot about Moira, leaving Offred with mixed feelings. We may appreciate the independent spirit that has helped her survive and her continuing contempt for authority. But, like Offred, we may regret that she has not played a more active role in some kind of rebellion against the enslaving system.

- The brothel name is another biblical allusion. Jezebel was the 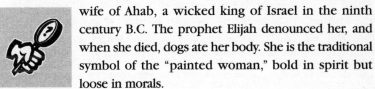 wife of Ahab, a wicked king of Israel in the ninth century B.C. The prophet Elijah denounced her, and when she died, dogs ate her body. She is the traditional symbol of the "painted woman," bold in spirit but loose in morals.

Chapter 39

Summary

The Commander and Offred ascend in a glass bubble elevator to one of the hotel rooms. Here, everything seems familiar and comforting to Offred. In the bathroom, she recalls something else Moira told her, that she had seen Offred's mother in the film about the Colonies. When Offred said she thought her mother was dead, Moira replied, "She might as well be." Offred wishes now she could remember the last time she saw her mother and what they might have talked about. When new restrictions were imposed and things became so much worse, Offred tried phoning her mother but could get no answer. She and Luke found her mother's apartment a vandalized wreck, but when Offred wanted to call the police, Luke warned her not to. Now Offred realizes that she must continue to mourn for her mother. She may still be alive in the Colonies but is dead as far as the world is concerned.

Offred looks at her tawdry reflection in the bathroom mirror and remembers she must be home by midnight to be "serviced" by Nick, according to Serena Joy's plan. Meanwhile, the Commander is waiting, and Offred lies down beside him. He reminds her that the next scheduled Ceremony is to be the following night, but says, "I thought we could jump the gun." She is cold to him, as he strokes her ankle where her identification tattoo indicates ownership by the state and by him. He tries to explain that he thought she might enjoy their sexual intimacy for a change.

The commander undresses and then begins to undress her. When she does not respond, he is disappointed. She tells herself that she knows how to fake a response, but admits that she can only be "inert," as she usually is during the Ceremony with him.

Commentary

• The image of Offred's mother in the Colonies, and Moira's blunt comment that she might as well be dead, adds another tragic note to Offred's story. She has thought often about her loved ones, now dead to her, but Moira's explanation about Unwomen makes her mother's fate almost unbearably real. As Offred says, "I've mourned for her already. But I will do it again, and again."

PART XIII • NIGHT • Chapter 40

Summary

Back in her room, Offred waits fully dressed until Serena Joy arrives at midnight. Offred follows her silently down to the empty kitchen, where Serena Joy whispers that she will wait for Offred's return. Offred wonders whether the Wife has bribed the sentries with cigarettes or whiskey.

Offred mounts the stairs to Nick's bachelor apartment over the garage. She knocks, and Nick appears in his shirt sleeves, smoking. Without preliminaries, he turns off the lamp and begins to undress her. As he kisses her, Offred says, "I can't wait . . . it's been so long, I'm alive in my skin, again" (p. 327). Then she admits that this reconstruction is not really how the incident happened. She creates the scene a second time, less romantically. She takes a drag on Nick's cigarette, becoming dizzy and feeling "stupid and ugly." Nick adopts an attitude of "punk surliness." Then they relax a little, exchanging sexual banter from old movie dialogue. The sadness of those lost times affects Offred, and Nick embraces her. "No romance," he says. Offred understands his meaning: no heroics, no risking of oneself for the other if they are caught. Then Offred admits that this version is also a reconstruction.

She says she is not sure, finally, exactly how the incident happened. She remembers thinking about Serena Joy sitting in the kitchen, perhaps thinking about "cheap" Handmaids who will do anything for a cigarette. Offred also remembers thinking that in responding to Nick's sexuality, she has betrayed her feelings for Luke. She says she would like to be completely innocent, ignorant of any shame in what she has done.

Commentary

• Offred confronts an old problem for story-tellers: **romance ver-**

sus realism. In traditional romance, heroic passions are exaggerated, and one-sided characters are good or evil, self-sacrificing or selfish. In realistic stories, emotions are subtle and characters more human, with conflicting values and shading in their motivations and actions. Offred's first version is a passionate scene in a darkened room, with a storm beginning outside. Her second is more realistic: two hesitant people in an awkward situation. The final version, the real one, was possibly too simple to have made an impression. Offred's mind wanders to more sordid details – Serena Joy's imagined thoughts about Handmaids, and her own feelings of betraying her husband Luke.

- Offred demonstrates how self-aware she has become after months of solitary self-analysis. The burden of self-awareness is heavy, and she would like to be free of shame or guilt about her reawakened sexuality.

PART XIV • SALVAGING • Chapter 41

Summary

After their first sexual encounter, Offred often goes back to Nick on her own, without Serena Joy's participation. And she does it for herself, feeling grateful each time that he lets her in. She becomes reckless, even crossing the lawn under the searchlights, expecting any moment to be gunned down. Nick might, for his own safety, have refused her, but he does not.

She describes a typical encounter. Nick welcomes her, closes the window, turns out the light. Offred quickly undresses. There is no time for talk. With the Commander, she closes her eyes, but with Nick she keeps them open. She wants to remember every detail, so she can "live on the image" later. She admits she ought to have done the same with Luke, but now he is fading from her memory.

Offred and Nick make love each time as if it will be their last. She feels safe with him, although they both know the risk they are taking. She dismisses her fears about trusting him completely. She talks about Moira and Ofglen, but not about Luke. She also avoids the subject of the Handmaid who hanged herself in her room, jealous that the other might also have visited Nick's bed. She tells him her real name. Nick says little, apparently content just having her body. Offred thinks it impossible that he could betray her. She thinks she is pregnant with his child, but admits it may be just wishful thinking. She wants him to be pleased, but they do not pursue the idea further.

Summer continues. On her walks, Offred pays little attention to Ofglen's whispered secrets. The activities of the underground are of no interest now that she has Nick. She is indifferent to Ofglen's suggestions that she might secretly go through the Commander's desk for information. Offred says she would be no good at spying, but it is really her own laziness that is speaking. Ofglen indicates that they could help her escape, but Offred admits to us that she no longer wants that. She would rather stay near Nick, she says, ashamed of herself. At the same time she feels this is a kind of boasting, demonstrating how serious this affair is for her. Some days she thinks more rationally, in terms of having settled into a comfortable way of life. Meanwhile, Ofglen gives up trying to get her cooperation, and Offred is relieved.

Commentary

- Offred is in love, although she does not use that word. She has reached an inactive stage in her character development , unchanging and complacent. As always, however, we are often reminded of the risks she is taking and may expect that she will soon face some new crisis.

- The romantic theme developed in this chapter - illicit lovers 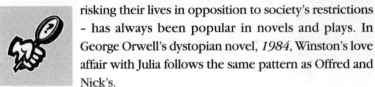 risking their lives in opposition to society's restrictions - has always been popular in novels and plays. In George Orwell's dystopian novel, *1984*, Winston's love affair with Julia follows the same pattern as Offred and Nick's.

Chapter 42

Summary

For a district Salvaging, a wooden stage has been erected on the lawn in front of the former university library. There are three posts with loops of rope, as well as a microphone at the front and a television camera off to one side. The audience consists of Wives and daughters at the back, Econowives and Marthas at the sides, and Handmaids kneeling in front on red cushions. From the stage, a long piece of rope runs back and forth on the ground through the audience rows. Two Handmaids and a Wife who are to be salvaged are seated on stage. Aunt Lydia heads the official procession, followed by two black-hooded Salvagers and several more Aunts. Offred tells us that this is only the second Salvaging she has attended. She does not want to be telling this story.

After conventional greetings, Aunt Lydia says that despite the unfortunate circumstances that bring them together, it is their duty to be here. Offred's mind wanders until Aunt Lydia announces that she will not, as usual, read out a long list of the prisoners' crimes. The Handmaids murmur their disapproval. The recital of crimes has been for them a kind of secret language, a way of knowing what they themselves might be capable of.

The Handmaid named Ofcharles is brought to the gallows, obviously drugged so that the ceremony will go smoothly. Offred hears a retching sound behind her, probably Janine being sick. Ofcharles is helped up onto a stool and hooded, with the noose around her neck. The stool is kicked away, and the two Salvagers drag downward with their full weight on Ofcharles' legs. Now the watching women lean forward, placing their hands on the thick rope that lies on the ground. Then each woman places a hand over her heart, demonstrating a symbolic participation in the actions of the Salvagers. Offred averts her eyes from the scene on stage.

Commentary

- Usually, the verb *to salvage* means to recover goods or materials from a disaster, such as shipwreck or fire. Atwood uses the word ironically. To the authorities of Gilead, it is an appropriate term for the *salvation* of criminals from their sins by means of public execution. Atwood is also suggesting that such a method of *salvation* is inhuman or *savage*.

Chapter 43

Summary

Aunt Lydia now tells the Handmaids to form a circle. Offred would rather keep back from whatever is to happen. She has heard, and only half believed, rumors about Particicutions. Two Guardians drag out a male prisoner, dirty and bruised, smelling of human waste and vomit. He has been convicted of brutally raping two Handmaids, one of whom lost her unborn child as a result. The penalty for rape is death.

Offred feels rising "bloodlust" for this man's violation of everything the Handmaids represent, but she knows she cannot touch him. When Aunt Lydia blows her whistle, and the Handmaids surge forward, Offred holds back. Ofglen rushes in first, pushing the criminal down and kicking him hard in the head. Then Offred's view is obscured by attacking Handmaids. When Ofglen rejoins her, Offred accuses her of savagery, but Ofglen tells her the victim was really a political subversive from Mayday. As an act of mercy, she knocked him out before the others got to him.

When Aunt Lydia signals a second time, the Guardians move in and pull the Handmaids away from what remains of the prisoner. Janine approaches Offred, her cheek smeared with blood, her eyes vacant of reason. She holds a clump of the victim's hair. She giggles as she wishes Offred "a nice day." Offred does not feel sorry for her, just angry. Nor is she proud of herself. She admits to being extremely hungry after the torrent of emotions she has experienced, and wonders whether this is her body's way of ensuring that she remain alive, able to repeat her "bedrock prayer: *I am, I am*."

Commentary

- In the Particicution, pressured by the crowd and her own "bloodlust," Offred almost forgets her usual restraint. Her emotions take her to the edge of unreason.
- The final appearance of Janine is a sad one. She has lost her "self" completely. The symbolic smear of blood, and her cheery words, demonstrate how totally she has been brainwashed by the system. Offred, however, maintains her own sense of "self" after the emotional draining. She can still state her firm conviction – "I

am" – and her heightened awareness that she must survive.

- Note the wordplay: *participation* and *execution* – Particicution. Atwood may have been thinking of "Participaction," a government-sponsored physical fitness movement of the 1970s.

- One mythological antecedent for the Particicution ceremony is in the Greek tragedy, *The Bacchae*, by Euripides (c. 408 B.C.). For sacrilege against the great god Dionysus, King Pentheus of Thebes is punished – torn apart by a group of the god's female devotees, including his own mother.

Chapter 44

Summary

The same afternoon, Offred goes to meet Ofglen as usual for shopping, noting Nick's crooked-hat signal as she passes. At the corner, the Handmaid who approaches her is not the Ofglen she expects, but a new one who greets Offred formally. Offred wonders how much of her loyalty and closeness to the former Ofglen she can reveal. Her new companion remains strictly formal, stating that she herself is Ofglen. This phrase means the former Ofglen, Offred's friend, has been removed.

After shopping, Offred suggests they go to the Wall, hoping to find out if the new Ofglen is also one of the underground. The morning's three victims hang there. Offred is aware that her senses are again alert and that she is taking large risks. She begins a simple conversation about the former Ofglen, using the word "Mayday" in passing. The new Ofglen responds with what seems to be a warning – she understands Offred's reference but is not herself part of the underground.

Offred is terrified that she has stupidly revealed too much. If Ofglen is a prisoner, she may be forced to reveal Offred's involvement. Offred worries about her missing loved ones, that they might be tortured in front of her. In a state of near panic, she realizes that if tortured, she would admit to anything. Then, just before the two Handmaids part, the new Ofglen quickly whispers that the former Ofglen hanged herself after the Salvaging, before the police van came to take her.

Commentary

- The sudden disappearance of Ofglen leaves Atwood's heroine on her own, and makes the dangers of resistance – even in so simple an act as knowing about the underground Mayday group – very real for Offred. Her terror about possible discovery has reawakened her commitment to survival. Once again she is more aware of her own situation and of missing her loved ones. The rush of fear that Ofglen's fate might be her own reaffirms the sense of "self" that she had temporarily set aside in loving Nick.

Chapter 45

Summary

Offred is so relieved, she promises God that she will give in completely. She knows she cannot ever embrace everything the Aunts and the authorities have tried to teach her. But she says it anyway, knowing that fear has made her realize for the first time how truly powerful the oppressive system is.

Before she can enter the house, Serena Joy calls to her and accuses her of betrayal. Offred remains silent. The Wife shows the cloak Offred wore to Jezebel's, and the flimsy, purple-sequined costume. "You could have left me something," she says, and Offred understands that perhaps Serena Joy does love her husband. The Wife continues: "Just like the other one. A slut. You'll end up the same."

Offred is aware that Nick, turning to look, has stopped whistling. She wants to go to him for protection but knows how stupid it would be to drag him down, too. She enters the house, "orderly and calm."

Commentary

- There are several implications in the words Serena Joy speaks. She indicates, for example, that she was aware of the Commander's activities with the previous Handmaid, and that she had warned him he was going too far in his private pleasures. In accusing Offred, she indirectly confirms the Handmaid's own ideas of how the Wives think of them as "sluts" who will do anything for small favors.

- This brief incident prepares us for the novel's climax in the next chapter.

PART XV • NIGHT • Chapter 46

Summary

In growing darkness, Offred waits at her window, holding the purple costume, feeling as if time has been suspended. She is calm, indifferent, holding on to the inscription scratched inside her closet: "Don't let the bastards grind you down."

She imagines several possibilities she might try to escape her fate, such as burning the house down or attacking Serena Joy. Or she could simply walk out of the door in her very visible red dress and see how far she might get before being arrested. The possibilities are of equal weight but little value; she will try none of them. Fatigue has overtaken her, and faith – in herself, in a useful exit or a future – is a meaningless word.

Offred imagines the other Handmaid, wearing the sequined costume and hanging from the chandelier. She thinks of her as a presence in the room, telling her, "There's no one you can protect, your life has value to no one."

She hears the approach of the black van before seeing its phosphorescent Eye insignia. Offred thinks that she has been wasting valuable time, that she might have stolen a kitchen knife or garden shears or knitting needles and been prepared to fight back. She hears heavy footsteps outside her door and is expecting a stranger to enter, but Nick comes in and turns on a light. Just when she is about to accuse him of being an Eye, he comes close and reassures her: "It's all right. It's Mayday. Go with them." She is suspicious. "Trust me," he says, and Offred realizes that trusting him is all she has left.

Two policemen from the van escort her downstairs. Outside the sitting room, Serena Joy asks what she has done, and Offred concludes that it was not the Wife who called them. The Commander asks to see a warrant and is told that "violation of state secrets" is involved. Offred can see that he is worried about what she might reveal about him. She can feel sorry for him, but his fear diminishes him in Offred's mind.

Serena Joy swears at Offred. Cora and Rita come from the kitchen, and Cora, who had hoped that Offred might bring a child to the household, is crying.

As Offred is helped into the van, she thinks, "Whether this is my end or a new beginning I have no way of knowing."

Commentary

- The novel's climax is unusual, for it leaves the plot unresolved. Since we are ostensibly reading Offred's first-person account, we must assume that after her arrest she reached some place of safety and was able to record her story. Nevertheless, her own doubts in the final sentences of this chapter seem real enough. Margaret Atwood's achievement is to have created so effective an impression of her protagonist that we have been taken in by the fiction. The realistic portrayal of a fully rounded human being, with all her self-confessed faults and fears, leaves us wondering about her fate and – like Offred herself – wanting to know "what's going on?"

HISTORICAL NOTES

Summary

The novel's final section, "Historical Notes on *The Handmaid's Tale*," is a transcript of the proceedings at an academic conference of professional historians. The setting is the University of Denay, in Nunavit, June 25, 2195. The historians have met to exchange ideas in the field of Gileadean Studies, and on this date the keynote speaker is Professor James Darcy Pieixoto of Cambridge University, England.

The transcript begins with polite introductions and several scholarly in-jokes – typical of university types who enjoy wordplay and clever literary and historical allusions. Then Professor Pieixoto begins his talk on "Problems of Authentication in Reference to *The Handmaid's Tale*."

He explains that the title, "The Handmaid's Tale," was given to Offred's account by Professor Knotly Wade when they co-edited the transcription of what Offred had left about 200 years ago: an audio diary discovered in what used to be Bangor, Maine, a prominent station on the Underground Femaleroad. Together, Pieixoto and Wade reconstructed the diary in the order that seemed to make best sense. Analysis by experts assured them that the tapes would have been very difficult to fake convincingly, and the editors turned their attention to authenticating the content of the tapes.

Pieixoto recognizes that Offred must have recorded the tapes some time after the events she tells of, when the necessary equipment was available and she had opportunity for the element of comment and reflection that runs through her account. To identify Offred herself, the editors tried to pinpoint the safe house in Bangor where she might have stayed while making the recordings. This investigation, however, led nowhere.

A second approach was to try to identify people who are prominent in the diary. Unfortunately, the authorities in Gilead routinely wiped out their own records when a purge of corrupt officials required a rewriting of history. Nevertheless, some records survived that were smuggled out of Gilead.

Pieixoto gives us some of the historical background for the establishment of Gilead. He explains why young mothers such as Offred were chosen as Handmaids and why the birthrate had fallen so drastically. Even before the Gilead period, common methods to raise the population had included artificial insemination, fertility clinics and the use of surrogate mothers. The Gileadean authorities outlawed the first two as irreligious but legitimized the third with biblical authority to back them. Hence the Handmaids.

From internal evidence in the diary itself, Pieixoto can discover no details that might identify Offred. Her physical characteristics, her age and her education reveal little. Similarly, the other names mentioned, "Luke," "Nick," "Moira" and "Janine" lead nowhere. They might be protective pseudonyms, supporting the idea that the tapes were made within the borders of Gilead while Offred was partway along in her escape.

Identifying "Commander Fred" might be more fruitful, and Pieixoto was able to narrow the possibilities to two candidates, Frederick R. Waterford, or B. Frederick Judd. Waterford had worked in market research and might have coined the words "Particicution" and "Salvaging" as used in Gilead. Judd was noted more for the actual tactics used in controlling the populace. He might have devised the form of the Particicution ceremony, knowing that the release of the Handmaids' pent-up hostility by tearing a man apart with bare hands was a useful way of scape-goating and getting rid of enemies. Judd might also have originated the idea of the Aunts, useful older women who could escape assignment to the Colonies by enforcing the Gileadean "traditional values" in Re-education Centers.

The attempt to identify the Wife of Commander Fred as "Serena Joy" was problematic. Waterford's and Judd's wives were named "Thelma" and "Bambi Mae" respectively. The name Offred uses may have been her own invention. Thelma had, however, once worked as a television evangelist. According to Pieixoto, this fact along with other evidence favors identifying Waterford as the Commander Fred in Offred's story. There is, for example, videotape evidence of Waterford's trial during one of the earliest Gileadean purges for corruption. He was accused of liberal tendencies, of having a large collection of heretical books and magazines and of harboring a subversive. The latter might have been Offred herself but was more likely Nick, a member of the Mayday underground and possibly a double agent, serving also as an Eye.

Pieixoto concludes by commenting that Offred's ultimate fate remains obscure. She might have been smuggled into Canada and from there to England. Then perhaps, fearing reprisals against Luke or her daughter, she might have quietly become a recluse, unwilling to make her story public. As for Nick, he might himself have been captured after assisting her escape, thus bringing about his own downfall out of devotion to her and the unborn child Offred was carrying.

Pieixoto concludes with a clever mythological analogy: Offred is like Eurydice, called back briefly from the dead but fading from existence before her story could be completely told.

Commentary

• Professor Pieixoto's discussion of his research methods and results provides additional background details about the history, organization and operation of the Gileadean regime. Nevertheless, the emphasis is still clearly focused on Offred's story and the possibilities of her redemption after escaping her oppressive situation.

- In these "Notes," Margaret Atwood continues in a satirical tone, but now it is for the sake of humor rather than political and sociological instruction. Her target is the kind of scholarly activity familiar to her from her own university career at Toronto and Harvard. The cheerful academic banter, the details of historical research methods, the unresolved conclusions after careful investigation and analysis are all gently ridiculed.
- Atwood also gets in one final pro-feminist dig at male chauvinist attitudes. Such attitudes have not changed in two hundred years, as illustrated by Pieixoto's joking comments about women – for example, punning on "Handmaid's Tale" and "tail."
- Professor Pieixoto's last line, "Are there any questions?" is Atwood's final touch of irony, directed at us. Of course there are!

Chapter Seven

Character sketches

Offred

Offred, the narrator, is the only character in the novel who changes and develops in response to her experiences. From the beginning, she is determined to survive the ordeal inflicted on her after the revolutionary coup that established the Republic of Gilead. Nevertheless, as she reveals more and more details of her own background and experiences new challenges to her integrity and sense of "self," she exposes her doubts and fears as a passive victim of the totalitarian regime. At the same time, she develops inwardly an independent, sometimes critical attitude about the system that enslaves her. At times she even risks becoming a sarcastic judge of others' behavior and an opportunistic exploiter of whatever advantages she can obtain.

Early influences: At an early age, Offred experienced firsthand her mother's militant feminism and was encouraged to participate in a public book-burning. However, because of the unsettled life in a one-parent family, by the time she was in her teens, she had come to disapprove of her mother's single-minded pursuit of the feminist cause. Her independence of spirit derived from her mother and at the same time developed in opposition to her mother.

At Harvard University, Offred enjoyed more independence of thought and action under the influence of her friend Moira. Here too, however, she somewhat prudishly disapproved of Moira's more outlandish behavior and her cynical attitudes about men. Then Offred entered a romantic stage, in her love affair with and later marriage to Luke, a university instructor. For several years, Offred worked in a library, enjoying life with Luke and making plans for a home and family.

The New Regime: The military-religious coup changed Offred's life entirely and began to change her settled character. She became, of necessity, more dependent on Luke and, at times, resentful of being so. A state of constant fear prevailed in her life, based on her awareness of pervasive spying and secret police, and on her concern for her mother and for Moira, both of whom were involved in unapproved, possibly illegal, political activities. In addition, the birth of Offred's daughter created a new urgency about escaping the oppressive rules of the Gileadean regime.

The Red Center: When Luke and their child disappeared from Offred's life at the time of their failed escape attempt, she went through a traumatic period of "lost time." While she was under the influence of drugs, the Aunts tried to recreate her character as a dutiful and obedient Handmaid in service to the state. Life at the Rachel and Leah Re-education Center was harsh, the rules strictly enforced. Constant reminders of biblical injunctions regarding the correct behavior and attitudes of child-bearing women like herself, along with the ritualized exercises, public humiliations and threats of punishment, almost succeeded in destroying Offred's sense of herself.

However, Offred retained much of her inner independence of thought and of the memories of her mother's and Moira's influence on her. Unlike Janine, for example, she did not give in to the brainwashing imposed by the Aunts. Although she participated in whatever was required of her, her need and desire to survive, to eventually recreate the life she had with Luke and their child in the time before, could not be brainwashed out of her. At the same time, she developed a critical, often sarcastically humorous attitude about the new social order.

Through the main part of the novel, it is these two elements, the need to survive and the critical attitude, that most clearly define Offred's character. The first provides the simple plot with its motivations; the second is, of course, Margaret Atwood's satirical approach to her subject, embodied in Offred.

Handmaid: Offred's intelligence and educational background are revealed in the many literary allusions that occur in her introspective examination of herself and her situation. Often she demonstrates a clever and humorous attitude, even when directing criticisms at herself. Her appreciation of wordplay, of puns and ambivalent meanings in words, is entirely appropriate in a world where reading is forbidden. An old word game like Scrabble has special significance for her, as a symbol of both longing for the past and present corruption undermining a position of high authority. At the same time, her critical judgment sees Scrabble games with the Commander as a bizarre ritual, imposed by a man whose motivations are sometimes adolescent and always puzzling to her.

Offred is sharply observant of every detail in the people around her, sensitive to the subtleties of their behavior despite the blinkered outlook imposed by her restrictive headdress. Her own sensual nature does not escape her close examination and sometimes self-deprecating humor. She longs for the romantic past, for a reunion with her husband, Luke, and life as it was before the catastrophe that led to their separation. She primes herself for romance, speculating about the Commander's true feelings for her, and watching Nick, the muscular Guardian-chauffeur, from her window. When she is given the opportunity for a liaison with Nick, she takes advantage of it, despite the risks. She blames herself for betraying her husband, but relaxes into the romantic moment-by-moment affair of guilty pleasure.

Escape: For a short time, Offred willingly loses her sense of self and naïvely trusts in her romantic feelings. She ignores the possibilities of rebellion or escape offered by Ofglen's contacts with the Mayday group. Then the possibility of new danger arises when Ofglen disappears. Offred regains her independence of spirit, her determination to survive. She takes the final risk, trusting Nick's assurances about Mayday, as she leaves the Commander's household for the last time.

Commander Fred (Frederick R. Waterford)

From the "Historical Notes," the last section of the novel, we know that Offred's Commander was probably Frederick R. Waterford who had a background in market research. He was responsible for the design of the Gileadean female costumes and particularly for red as the Handmaids' color. He may have originated the term "Particicution" and probably initiated the idea of Salvagings – including the rope ceremony – as the public method of exterminating political enemies. Waterford also implemented the idea of the Aunts as efficient teachers and disciplinarians for the Handmaids in training. He even suggested reassuring names derived from familiar commercial products – cosmetics, cake mixes, medicinal remedies – for the Aunts themselves. He was an ingenious contributor to the philosophy and practices of early Gilead.

As Offred knows him, he is at first a shadowy figure, the object of her resentment and hatred because of what he represents: the enslaving authority that controls every feature of her life. His puzzling behavior when she unexpectedly encounters him outside her room begins a change in her – and our – understanding of his character. In the Ceremony, he asserts his leadership role first by keeping Serena Joy and the others waiting, then by knocking at and entering the sitting room without waiting for the usual formal invitation. He leads the first part of the Ceremony, reading from the Bible and calling for silent prayer. In the bedroom episode, he is detached, performing his sexual duty mechanically, without apparent emotional involvement with either Offred or Serena Joy.

When he requires Offred's presence in his private study, he begins to reveal his inner self. He is much like a young adolescent trying too hard on a first date, showing off a little for Offred's benefit how he can get away with breaking rules. He seems to want her interest and her approval. When he requests that she play Scrabble with him, he shows that, like her, he longs for familiar activities of the past, intellectual stimulation of a basic, somewhat juvenile kind. His interest in books and magazines, and in the words they create together in the Scrabble games, shows a mind at play, enjoying what is now forbidden but was once a part of everyday life.

He also reveals a sincere desire for some emotional return from Offred, a personal contact that he no longer has with his wife, Serena Joy. The clandestine visit to Jezebel's takes this a step further. Again, he wants to show off to Offred and show her off to others of his own rank. At the same time, he admits it is an experiment to find out whether the sexual relations between them can be enjoyed in a situation far removed from the formal, approved ritual of the monthly Ceremony.

In conversations with Offred, he reveals a sincere commitment to the philosophy and practices of Gilead. He was one of its founders, a member of the Sons of Jacob Think Tanks, and is now a high authority in the ruling hierarchy. His loyalty to the system is real, although his defense of it, particularly as regards the role of women, seems weak and self-serving to Offred and to us. Moira comments that the Commander's exploitation of Offred, by bringing her in makeup and sequined costume to Jezebel's, is "just another crummy power trip." This is a convenient summation from the feminist point of view Moira represents; but behind the power trip is a more complex character, sometimes a little pathetic and often confusing to Offred.

Frederick B. Waterford, we are told, was eliminated shortly after Offred's departure in one of the earliest Gileadean purges. He was accused of liberal tendencies, of hoarding heretical magazines and books and of harboring a subversive.

Serena Joy

Offred remembers Serena Joy from a television show in the late 1960s called the *Growing Souls Gospel Hour*. The Commander's Wife was then a singer called "Pam," who was so emotionally involved in the performance of hymns and Bible stories for children that she could smile and cry real tears at the same time. Later, she became an advocate for the traditional values of home and family, making speeches and giving interviews to news magazines. Clashes between feminist and anti-feminist supporters were heating up in the late '70s, and led to more than one assassination attempt on Serena Joy's very public life.

Now, as the Wife of Commander Fred, she is crippled by an arthritic leg and bitter about her confinement as a Wife, about her lack of children and about the need for Handmaids. She is determined to maintain her marriage and her control of the household. In spring and summer, she spends time in her garden, tending flower beds dug for her by a Guardian detailed to the Commander's service. Indoors, her domain is the sitting room, where she sits and smokes black market cigarettes, her leg propped on a footstool, knitting elaborately patterned scarves for Angels on the front lines. Offred thinks the scarves may be just busy-work for the Wives, but she envies Serena Joy the activity, the challenges and small goals of these knitting projects. She is aware of the Wife's bitterness and discontent. Sometimes she hears the sound of pacing from the sitting room, back and forth, each heavy step followed by the light tap of Serena Joy's cane. Sometimes she hears the Wife's voice, a thin singing at low volume from a recording made long ago before her glory faded.

On evenings of the Ceremony, Serena Joy asserts her authority by impatiently pointing out how the Commander, as usual, keeps the others waiting. She controls the television set as they wait, allowing brief glimpses of typical televangelist programs and the latest war news or official propaganda about captured subversives. During the first part of the Ceremony, she can still shed real tears, probably for her own situation as what Aunt Lydia would call a "defeated woman," when the Commander reads the biblical handmaid story of Jacob and Rachel. During the ritualized intercourse between the Commander and Offred, Serena Joy, in her symbolic participation, firmly controls Offred's passive posture. She is relieved when the ritual is finished, and, perhaps out of jealousy, dismisses Offred as soon as the Commander has left the bedroom.

Serena Joy is naturally resentful of this need for Offred as potential child-bearer, but her desire for a child – like that of all the Wives – is strong. Cunningly, with the promise of a photograph purported to be of Offred's daughter, she tempts the Handmaid into taking the great risk of a sexual encounter with Nick. To Offred, it seems to be Serena Joy's usual method, probably tried with previous Handmaids. It is a necessary element in the system.

However, when the Wife finds evidence of Offred and the Commander's evening excursion to Jezebel's, her anger and resentment erupts. She complains bitterly about this betrayal in her marriage situation. "I trusted you. I tried to help you," she says to Offred. "You could have left me something." It is the complaint of a defeated woman.

Moira

Offred's best friend at university presents a side of the female character that Offred admires and appreciates: "quirky, jaunty, athletic . . . irreverent, resourceful." Moira enjoys risks taken for simple amusement or for the sake of independence from outside control. At the same time, Offred expresses her disapproval of Moira's more extreme activities, such as the "underwhore party," modelled on a Tupperware party but for sexy underwear.

After university, Moira worked in the publishing division of the women's movement. She admired Offred's mother for her feminist principles and developed her own cynical attitudes about men and male-dominated society. When the revolutionary coup took place, Moira and others like her went underground with their illegal activities, writing and printing their materials in basements and back rooms. She was eventually arrested by the authorities, and the printing press was destroyed. Like Offred, she was taken to the Red Center for re-education.

Moira demonstrated her resourcefulness in her first attempt to escape from the Red Center. She faked an illness, hoping that a trip to hospital might lead to freedom. She even had the idea that the two Guardians accompanying her in the ambulance would be eager for sexual favors and might help. When she was brought back, despite the physical torture that made her unable to walk for a week, her spirit was not broken.

When Janine came close to a complete breakdown at the Red Center, the result of her too willing compliance with Aunt Lydia's dominance and her own public humiliation and self-abasement, it was Moira who pulled her back to reality. She told the others how to treat Janine if it should happen again when Moira was not there. Offred concluded from this that Moira was already planning a second break-out attempt.

The second escape attempt was even more resourceful than the first and involved the physical restraint of Aunt Elizabeth and a disguise in the Aunt's clothing. Moira almost succeeded in escaping to Canada with the help of the Underground Femaleroad. To the other Handmaids, says Offred, Moira was a heroic fantasy, a dangerous "loose woman" attempting to control her own fate.

When Moira turns up at Jezebel's, she seems satisfied in being characterized as an "incorrigible" and in serving as a prostitute. Her choice was to avoid being sent as an Unwoman to the Colonies, and at Jezebel's she found opportunities to use the system to her own advantage. Access to cosmetics, drugs and lesbian companions are perhaps the best that someone like Moira could ever expect in Gilead. She remains a hard-headed realist, facing the truths about herself, about the fate of Offred's mother in the Colonies and about Offred's situation with the Commander.

Offred's final comment is that she would like to be able to tell how Moira committed some outrageous and heroic act, such as blowing up Jezebel's while fifty Commanders were inside. That would be typical of Moira, but unfortunately, says Offred, it did not happen, and she never saw Moira again.

Throughout the novel, Moira represents the rebellious spirit of early 1970s feminism. She is an example of the independent women who inherited their ideas and ideals from the feminist pioneers, from women like Offred's mother.

Offred's mother

The character of Offred's mother is defined by her active partic-ipation in the women's movement from the 1960s onwards. One of Offred's earliest memories is of a magazine-burning celebration in a park. Her mother had taken over their usual Saturday time together to meet with her friends in the public protest against exploitation of women in sex magazines. She tried to protect young Offred from seeing the magazine illustrations of bound female victims, but she wanted Offred to participate in burning the materials.

In a film shown at the Red Center, what Aunt Lydia called an "Unwoman documentary," Offred saw her mother at an earlier time, before she herself was born. Her mother was young, laughing, optimistic and energetic, dressed in overalls, plaid shirt and sneakers. She was a sincere and self-confident protester, earnest in her commitment, carrying a banner in a parade, demanding safety for women on the streets and freedom of choice in regard to abortion. She was 37 years old, when Offred was born, a single mother by choice. She always insisted that Offred was very much a wanted child. She had little more than contempt for men like Offred's father, although as she aged into a spunky, wiry, gray-haired nonconformist, she sometimes tearfully admitted to being lonely in her pursuit of feminist principles.

She had a sly wit and cockiness, a playfully scornful way of joking with Luke after he and Offred were living together. She would accuse them of not truly understanding how much the women like herself had sacrificed to bring about the sexual equality they enjoyed in their marriage. But this was just before the revolution occurred, and later, when Offred and Luke tried to contact her, they found only her ransacked apartment. Her long-standing and energetic activism in women's issues had made her an enemy of the new state.

Offred's last information about her mother comes from Moira at Jezebel's. Moira had been shown a film of life in the Colonies, where Offred's mother, now an Unwoman, was living out her final few years. She might as well be dead, says Moira, and Offred mourns again for the mother she had never completely approved of, who had enjoyed being more outrageous, more of a rebel than her daughter.

Janine (Ofwarren)

While Moira and Offred's mother represent one end of a spectrum in regard to female independence and self-fulfillment, Janine represents the other end. At the Red Center, she had been easily won over by Aunt Lydia and the other Aunts. In Testifying, Janine humiliated herself with self-accusations of having been at fault when she was once gang-raped and had an abortion. The story might not even have been true, according to Offred, but it was Janine's way of fitting in, of seeking Aunt Lydia's approval by such self-abasement. At prayers she was one of those who got emotionally worked up, crying and moaning. Even Aunt Lydia warned her about making a spectacle of herself.

Offred and the others despised Janine for her pale, tearful weakness, although they could see how her Testifying was part of the brain-washing that defeated them as individuals. On one occasion,

Janine lost touch with reality, reliving memories of her past life when she was a server in a restaurant. It was Moira who helped her, slapping her back into the present and warning the others that they must do the same if Janine should ever go off the edge like that again.

After Moira's successful escape, Janine became Aunt Lydia's pet and accomplice in spying on the other women. She passed on the Aunt's story of Moira's outrageous crimes, but the others never trusted her and avoided her when possible.

When Offred later encounters Janine, now Ofwarren, on a shopping excursion, she is clearly showing off her pregnancy for the benefit of the other Handmaids. Her smirking awareness of her success and their failure is obvious. At the Birth Day ceremony, Janine's baby is at first welcomed as a triumph to be shared by all the Handmaids. Later, when the infant is pronounced an Unbaby, Janine's character – or what is left of it – disintegrates.

Offred encounters her again. At the Salvaging, Ofglen suggests that the sound of retching is Janine's reaction to the executions they are witnessing. Later, after the Particicution, Janine approaches Offred with a cheery smile and greeting, clutching a handful of the male victim's blond hair. "She's let go," says Offred, "totally now, she's in free fall, she's in withdrawal." In her loss of self, Janine is far removed from the self-aware and independent spirit represented by Moira and by Offred's mother. Obviously Atwood is suggesting that the conformist role is ultimately barren and self-destructive.

Aunt Lydia

Throughout the main part of Offred's memoir, we learn how important Aunt Lydia is in the structure of the Handmaid system. She is one of several Aunts who, armed with electric cattle prods, enforce strict discipline among the Handmaids in training, through public humiliation, punishment and torture. She wears a khaki uniform, and round, steel-rimmed spectacles. Her teeth protrude a little, long and yellowish, reminding Offred of the teeth of rodents caught by her pet cat in the time before. When Aunt Lydia occasionally laughs at one of her own jokes, it is a "heldback neighing," something not quite natural or even human to Offred's ear.

Aunt Lydia soon emerges as the Handmaids' principal teacher.

She is "in love with either/or," says Offred, suggesting that Aunt Lydia allows no compromises within the Handmaid system: you are either for it, or against it, and should therefore accept the privilege and status as given. She demonstrates a firm commitment to her job, even when she occasionally shows a simple, motherly attitude and more human emotions toward her "girls." She sometimes wrings her hands, seeming nervous and pleading, her voice trembling in her instructions to the young women. But she does it to emphasize arguments about their proper behavior and attitudes toward men and toward the Wives with whom they will be so closely associated. The Handmaids are careful not to react when Aunt Lydia is touched by her own memories and emotions. She might appear "abstracted," says Offred, "but she was aware of every twitch" among her pupils. Reprisals could be cruel.

Aunt Lydia is fond of contrasting the present situation with the past. She states that there are two kinds of freedom, "freedom to and freedom from." In what she calls "the days of anarchy," women were free to indulge in every form of sexual vice and deviance, preventing pregnancies and having abortions, always at risk of male dominance and often violence. Now they are free from such perversions and dangers, although they are required to conform to the limitations of the Handmaid's veil and the restricted life it represents. Aunt Lydia emphasizes that the present system will become "ordinary" to the Handmaids, and she is right to some extent. Even Offred admits that she has come to feel secure within the limitations of her Handmaid's life, despite her admiration for, and envy of, the rebellious heroism of someone like her friend Moira. Aunt Lydia looks forward to a time when Handmaids will "accept their duties with willing hearts" and will find their lives easier, because "they won't want things they can't have."

On a practical level, Aunt Lydia is an efficient manager. When Moira escapes from the Red Center, Aunt Lydia exploits Janine's self-confessed weaknesses, making her a pet and spy. At the Prayvaganza described by Offred, Aunt Lydia oversees, announcing a change in procedures regarding the listing of the current victims' crimes, and directing the executions of three condemned women. In the Particicution that follows, she encourages the anger and hatred of the Handmaids against the condemned man, and with her whistle, controls the bloody dismemberment of the victim. We might suspect that she is also responsible for the accusations against Ofglen that lead to the latter's suicide before being arrested by the secret police.

Aunt Lydia believes that "The Republic of Gilead knows no bounds . . . . Gilead is within you." This statement defines her character, her commitment to what she believes have been victories for women, to what she now trains them for even when cruelty and deceit are required.

Luke

Offred's husband was a university instructor when they began their relationship. He was married at the time, and the two met secretly and romantically in hotel rooms, until he divorced his wife and married Offred. They were a loving and contented couple, dreaming of a home and children in an upscale residential area of the city.

Offred used to tease Luke about being pedantic when he showed off his learning by explaining Latin origins of words or the use of "Mayday" as a distress signal. Whatever arguments they had were minor, enjoyable from Offred's later perspective, although she recalls one more serious occasion after the birth of their daughter. Luke objected to Offred's saving of plastic shopping bags. He worried that they might pose a danger of suffocation if their child, playing, got one over her head. Ironically, the family must ultimately deal with much greater dangers.

When they watched Serena Joy on television, as she preached about traditional family values, tears in her eyes and her heavy mascara staining her cheeks, Luke thought her funny, but Offred found the woman's earnestness a little frightening. Luke took little serious interest in feminist issues or reactions to the women's movement and would tease Offred's mother about the differences between men and women that gave men dominance. He dominated in the marriage, and when the revolutionary coup took place and women's employment and financial independence were taken away, Offred suspected that Luke approved. The new situation meant he was in control of the family's life. The balance between them had shifted, says Offred, and she now felt dependent on Luke's more dominant role in their marriage.

Before their attempt to escape across the border to Canada, it was Luke who realized the dangers of leaving their cat behind to call attention to their absence. He "took care of it," meaning that he objectified the pet, made it a "thing" to be disposed of, something that Offred could not have done.

They were betrayed at the border checkpoint, despite careful planning and Luke's outward display of optimism. Later, Offred imagines three possibilities for her husband's end: he was shot dead in the woods; he was captured, imprisoned, tortured by the Eyes; or – and this is where her hope lies – he successfully escaped and joined with the resistance movement, from where he would eventually get a message back and finally rescue her. Offred's belief in Luke as defender and protector, and her continuing loyalty to the love they shared, sustains her in many private moments of near-despair.

Nick

Although Nick plays an active role in Offred's story of her time at the Commander's home, we know little about his character. Offred at first sees him as a cocky, somewhat privileged Guardian assigned to the household, one who cheerfully takes risks in winking at her or speaking to her. Offred wonders about his apparent indifference to his low status, his lack of connection. She thinks there may be more to him, that perhaps he is really a member of the secret police.

During the first part of the Ceremony Offred describes, he imposes his attentions on her, by secretly nudging his boot against her foot. Later the same evening, when she meets him alone in the sitting room, they are both attracted by the possibility of sharing more than an embrace. There is a spark of passionate desire on both sides, although they are sensible enough of the dangers to let the moment go.

Nick becomes the go-between for the Commander's secret meetings with Offred, adjusting his chauffeur's cap as signal to her when she is expected to go to the Commander's study. Offred wonders what Nick gets out of this arrangement; perhaps it is just knowing that he has something on her, or enjoying a small sense of power over the Commander and his secret activities. When he drives them to Jezebel's, Offred wonders what Nick thinks of her, whether he disapproves or is angry, lustful or jealous of the

Commander's use of her.

Serena Joy arranges the first secret meeting between Offred and Nick, and Offred tries out various "reconstructions" to describe the beginning of their love affair. She settles on a down-to-earth, realistic description. Both are hungry for sex, and the risks involved do not dissuade them from settling into a pattern of repeated late night meetings. Offred learns to trust Nick, telling him much about her life and even her real name, although he offers no information about himself or his thoughts. Offred mentions "his long sardonic unrevealing face," suggesting perhaps that there is depth to Nick's character that she cannot know. Nevertheless, she feels safe with him when they are making love.

When Offred leaves the Commander's household for the last time, it is Nick, as double agent, who may have called in the Eyes to remove her. Since Ofglen's connection with Mayday has been discovered, Nick possibly sees his own safety in jeopardy. On the other hand, it may be Nick who arranged for Offred to be rescued by the Mayday organization. Nick's ultimate fate and role is unknown.

Ofglen

When Ofglen first appears in the story, she has been Offred's shopping partner for only two weeks. The previous companion on the daily excursion (who would also have been called Ofglen) was simply replaced, without explanation. This second Ofglen is also replaced without explanation about six months later, just before the story's climax.

The second Ofglen is initially formal in the accepted ways, with the proper greeting and good-bye each time she and Offred meet. She maintains her Handmaid's "invisibility" always, modestly keeping her head down, tucking her gloved hands up into her sleeves. She regularly suggests a visit to the churchyard, where she stands as if praying. Offred judges her "as a woman for whom every act is done for show." Offred does note, however, that in viewing bodies hanging on the Wall, Ofglen seems to suppress a tremor of emotion, tears possibly for the executed victims.

It turns out there is good reason for Ofglen's "show" of complete conformity. After several weeks, she takes the risk of using the code word "Mayday" in conversation with Offred, but gets no response. The two women become more comfortable with each other, dropping the usual formalities as they follow their daily shopping routine together. Then finally, outside Soul Scrolls, Ofglen take a huge risk with treasonous questions about God and the effectiveness of prayer. This time Offred does respond, and Ofglen explains secretly that she is in touch with the resistance movement. She invites Offred to be part of the Mayday group.

At the Prayvaganza described by Offred, Ofglen reveals an ironic side to her nature much like Offred's own, commenting sarcastically about the presiding Commander's biblical reference on the need for sobriety among women. Following the session, she pumps Offred for information about Commander Fred, hoping the Mayday group can make use of anything she might provide. But after Offred begins her affair with Nick, and shows less interest in contacts with the resistance movement, Ofglen tells her that escape might be possible. They can "get people out" in cases of immediate danger, but at this time Offred wants only to stay with Nick.

During the Particicution that follows the Salvaging ritual, Ofglen shows how far she will go to maintain her own cover, while at the same time assisting the Mayday group. As the enraged Handmaids close in on the accused rapist, Ofglen is first to attack, pushing him to the ground and kicking him savagely in the head. Offred accuses her of barbarism, but Ofglen – still maintaining her show of conformity – warns that the Aunts are watching. She quickly explains that the victim was one of their own, a political resistance fighter, and she had put him out of his misery by knocking him unconscious before the others tore him limb from limb.

Later the same day, Ofglen disappears, and Offred meets the third of that name for the usual shopping trip. The new Ofglen is formal, correct, unwilling to respond to Offred's reference to Mayday. But she does reveal that her predecessor committed suicide before she could be taken away by the secret police. The former Ofglen sacrificed herself before she could be tortured into betraying the resistance movement, and that final commitment and "escape" bring Offred back to an awareness of her own danger.

Chapter Eight

Plot structure

Margaret Atwood's structuring method in *The Handmaid's Tale* is to provide three story lines, three perspectives and three ways of approaching her characters and themes. The first two are Offred's – her activities in the present and her meditations on the past changes in the social context that have created the Republic of Gilead. The third is the historical "frame," a perspective from 200 years after Offred's time.

Offred's personal story

The main plot of *The Handmaid's Tale* is simple enough, covering a period of about six months, from early spring to early autumn, during the third year of the narrator's life as a Handmaid. In longer sections of several chapters each, Offred describes various aspects of life in the Republic of Gilead. Beginning with her own restricted world, the Commander's household and her place in it, she gradually expands our knowledge and understanding of Gileadean society. We learn of the regular routines of daily shopping and the monthly Ceremony of ritualized mating, as well as the less common rituals of Birth Days, Prayvaganzas and Salvagings. Throughout, we are also given brief "memory associations," images and incidents recalled from Offred's life before her present situation.

Offred begins meeting privately with the Commander; she learns from her shopping partner that there is an underground resistance movement at work; she plots with her Commander's Wife to try for pregnancy through a secret sexual liaison with the Commander's chauffeur; she is exposed as a traitor to her Commander and his Wife. The climax occurs when she is taken away in a secret police van, trusting that her captors are subversives who will deliver her to the safety of the resistance group. In addition, there are two contrasting subplots. Moira is Offred's best friend from university days, a natural rebel who accommodates her individuality to the authoritarian regime by exploiting its weaknesses. Janine is a weak-willed Handmaid who eventually loses completely her sense of self and her reason to the demands of the authorities in power.

Social context

The longer sections alternate with one-chapter sections labelled "Night" (and in one case, "Nap"). In these, Offred usually takes time to reflect on her experiences and relive in greater detail incidents from the past. In this way, she fills in the contrasting world of life before the Gileadean regime forcibly assumed power.

We learn about her childhood and her feminist mother's participation in the women's movement, her university career, her marriage and – most significantly – her attempted escape from growing totalitarian oppression after the revolutionary coup and her capture and assignment to the Handmaid program. The story of her life during the time with Commander Fred is set within this context, so that while we follow Offred's limited, day-to-day activities, we are always aware of the traces of the past that survive in the harsh reality of the present.

Historical frame

The author then adds an additional context, the "Historical Notes," which are the novel's final section. This simple "frame" story is set 200 years after Offred's. Professor Pieixoto, speaking to a conference of historians at a northern university in A.D. 2195, explains how *The Handmaid's Tale* came to be. We learn that Offred's story was reconstructed from an audio tape diary or memoir and that the experts have been at pains to authenticate the tapes and identify the historical personages behind Offred's descriptions of Commander Fred and his Wife.

In diagram form, the plot structure looks like this:

**Offred as Handmaid
In household of Commander Fred,
April - September, c.1988**

**The Time Before
Offred's birth, c.1955 / military coup, c.1980
/ escape attempt, c.1985 /
Red Center and previous postings, c.1985-1988**

**Nunavit Conference, A.D. 2195
Reconstruction of Offred's
audio tape diary**

The effect of this structure is to present a convincing picture of a totalitarian society and one individual's struggle to survive oppression, hardship, cruelty and danger. The picture accumulates gradually, but by the end of the novel, we have a believable and fully rounded character to appreciate, and a strong theme statement about the indomitable human spirit that can survive any oppressive system.

Chapter Nine

Setting

Margaret Atwood uses three main settings that correspond to the three parts of her plot structure. Once again, the first two are observed from Offred's perspective, while the third involves the frame story, looking back from 200 years in the future.

Household

Offred's immediate surroundings, the home of Commander Fred and Serena Joy, is in an upscale residential area of Cambridge, Massachusetts. The residence is large and includes a separate above-garage room for the chauffeur, Nick, and servants quarters for the Marthas, Rita and Cora. The Commander and Serena Joy have their private, restricted areas – office and sitting-room, respectively. Offred's sparsely decorated room overlooks the driveway and garage. Through the shatterproof glass of her window, she can see the sentries and, at night, searchlights maintaining security. Offred and Ofglen walk to the shopping area through residential streets lined with similar homes, an area that is apparently empty of children.

Cambridge, Massachusetts, is the site of Harvard University (where Atwood did post-graduate studies at Radcliffe College in the 1960s) and is linked by subway to Boston. Offred and Ofglen's shopping excursions often take them close to the university campus. Later incidents, notably the "Salvaging" episode, take place beyond the "Wall," within the former university grounds. The university setting is symbolically significant. What was once a place of learning, of intellectual freedom for open discussion, analysis and criticism, is now the headquarters of the most impenetrable and cruelly powerful element in the social structure, the secret police or "Eyes."

Society

The social hierarchy of the Commander's household is itself a microcosm of the larger society. Offred, as Handmaid, is placed below the status of the Wife, Serena Joy, at a level perhaps equivalent to Nick, the trusted chauffeur. Offred is above the servant-class Marthas, but she also stands somewhat apart from the hierarchical "chain" of status by virtue of her role as breeder in a potentially sterile society. The social structure of Gilead illustrates the same pyramidic pattern: the political powers, Commanders, vaguely defined in their actual duties and activities, are at the top; the others are ranked below them, down to the Unwomen in the Colonies at the bottom. (See the "Color symbolism" box p. 129 in the section on "Style.") As Offred fills in details of her daily domestic routines, she gradually sketches a picture of the whole, carefully structured and controlled society.

Atwood has chosen her principal New England setting with historical and symbolic significance in mind. New England was the so-called "cradle" of the American War of Independence in the 1770s. Salem, Massachusetts, not far from Boston, was the site of the witchcraft scare of the 1690s, when severe religious authorities executed at least twenty victims, whose non-conformist beliefs and activities condemned them under strict Puritan laws. In the time of the story, the residential district of Cambridge is "the heart of Gilead" according to Offred (p. 29), possibly suggesting that Commander Fred is close to the center of the country's political power.

The actual borders of the Republic of Gilead are never defined. We are given a few suggestions about the outside world. For example, the New England area is a convenient one for potential escape, with access to the "Underground Femaleroad" that might take runaway Handmaids across the border into Canada. There are Japanese tourists on the local streets, Arab businessmen at Jezebel's and dark references to the Colonies where Unwomen live out their brief, dying years. But the outside world is no clearer an image to us than it can be to Offred, with her limited perspective symbolically restricted by the headdress she wears.

Atwood's novel was published in 1985. Unlike Huxley in *Brave New World*, Orwell in *1984*, or Bradbury in *Fahrenheit 451*, she has not set her main story in the distant, or even the near future. (See

"Fictional dystopias" chart, p. 121.) Instead, she has rewritten the immediate past – the years from about 1975 to 1985 – to exploit real current events, especially the feminist movement and the backlash it aroused, along with a growing right-wing religious movement. These cultural elements become important influences in the creation and early development of the Republic of Gilead, from about 1980 onward in Atwood's time scheme. By 1988, when Offred is at her third posting as Handmaid in Commander Fred's household, Gileadean society is firmly in place, though still fighting to maintain its borders against unspecified outside forces. By projecting only a little way beyond 1985 into the immediate future, Atwood emphasizes the threats she sees to the stability and freedoms of her contemporary society.

Frame

The setting of the frame story is far removed in both geography and time from Offred's tale. The academic "Symposium on Gileadean Studies" takes place in the far north, at the University of Denay, Nunavit, on June 25, 2195, about 200 years after Offred's time.

This setting allows Atwood several ironic effects. We are to understand that cultural and climatic changes have occurred over the previous two hundred years. The delegates to the conference enjoy recreational excursions for fishing, nature walks and an "Outdoor Period-Costume Sing-Song" (p. 372). The suggestion is that global warming has made the Arctic a temperate zone and perhaps devastated the American south and equitorial areas.

More important, by looking back 200 years, the keynote speaker, Professor Pieixoto, establishes an outsider's perspective – corresponding to our own – on the events described in Offred's tale, and on Gileadean society itself, including suggestions of the Republic's eventual downfall. Pieixoto's analysis is detailed but maintains a detached, ironic, amused tone that Atwood seems to want her readers to enjoy, despite the main story's dark realities. In other words, the author uses the frame setting and incident to guide us effectively to relevant interpretations of character and theme. We are also reassured, to some extent, that Offred survives and Gilead falls – a happy ending, of sorts.

Chapter Ten

Themes

A story's **themes**, its **universal truths**, often express the author's point of view about life. Several important themes in *The Handmaid's Tale* may be categorized in three groups: (1) the microcosm – the small world of Offred's personal struggle within the limited scope of her immediate situation; (2) the macrocosm – the larger world of the Gileadean social structure, where the male-female power struggle dominates; and (3) the frame – the outsider's historical perspective, as well as the author's own creative process.

These three groupings, and their relationship to the novel's structure, may be represented by the following diagram. (Compare the similar diagram illustrating "Plot Structure" on page 110.)

The microcosm:
Offred's internal struggle
The ondomitable human spirit
and the integrity of "self"

The macrocosm: Gileadean social structure?
personal choice / feminist Issues
who has power / control?

The frame: historical notes
the creative process / reconstruction
Margaret Atwood as literary guide

Themes in the microcosm

The indomitable human spirit

Despite Offred's oppressive situation, Margaret Atwood expects us from the beginning of her novel to recognize the human spirit's ability to resist attempts at control or suppression.

At the center of Offred's story is her continuing insistence that she will survive. She wants to get through this oppressive ordeal and, she hopes, be reunited with her husband and daughter. As the Sufi proverb given in an epigraph at the beginning suggests, there is little in Gilead to sustain the human spirit, but what little there is may, through faith and hope, be transformed into nourishment, "bread" from the stones of the desert. Ultimately, Offred has faith in herself.

The integrity of "self"

Closely related is the need to retain one's sanity, one's sense of "self," without betraying principles of self-awareness and honesty.

Unlike Janine, Moira, her mother and other female victims of the Gileadean patriarchal system, Offred manages to escape with her reason and her uncompromising honesty about herself intact. Although she briefly loses sight of this commitment to herself during the time of her affair with Nick, the danger of exposure and arrest after Ofglen's suicide brings her back to her central purpose: to survive.

 ## Self-awareness and honesty

A broader application of the **integrity of self theme** is evident in Atwood's other works, notably in her non-fiction study of Canadian literature, *Survival*. Atwood sees Canadian literature as a product of the unique features of the landscape and the historical struggle for survival. The sense of self-awareness and honesty in Canadian writers derives from the difficulties of nourishing a culture in a hostile wilderness environment.

Themes in the macrocosm

Personal choice

In Gileadean society, power – who has control over his or her own life – is an important thematic thread. Power is determined by how much choice any individual has in making personal decisions.

Offred comments in Chapter 5 about the dangers of having choices, and life without choice has for her almost become "ordinary," another of Aunt Lydia's comments (p. 43) on the strength of this society with its rules and controls. Offred's struggle involves personal choice – to give in to or to rebel against Gilead's stringent restrictions. She struggles daily with the limitations of forced conformity and the possibilities of rebellion. Offred's conflict can be illustrated in chart form:

FORCES OF OUTWARD CONFORMITY	*VS*	SOURCES OF INNER REBELLION
• Ignorance of real events • Fear of punishment		• Hope for survival • Faith in her essential sanity

Feminist issues

In the society of Offred's time, some limited feminist goals have been won, but at the cost of personal freedoms.

The women's movement of the 1960s and 1970s identified and targeted for change the male-dominated, patriarchal social structure, in politics, business and everyday life. Like those feminists, Aunt Lydia might look forward to a time when all women "will live in harmony together . . . . united for a common end!" (p. 203). But the end, in Aunt Lydia's view, is maintaining the male-dominated power structure, creating the "ordinary" by rebuilding and indoctrinating the population. The Gileadean power structure makes the streets safe for women, frees them from sexual harassment or violence and ensures proper respect for the status of Wives and Handmaids. But this new patriarchal system with its guarantees for women is not exactly what Offred's mother and her activist friends had in mind.

Who has power/control?

Power and control in Offred's world mean exploiting one's position in the social hierarchy by exerting shrewd influence over others.

Three forms of power are evident: (1) the Commanders' political and military control in the running of society; (2) the Wives' control over "women's business" – everything to do with the role of the Handmaid in the household and in the procreation of children; and (3) the exertion of power by individuals through bribes and exchanges of favors, or through risky personal choices.

As a fictional dystopia, Gilead most prominently depicts the power structure of the Handmaid system and the social and political controls that restrict freedoms. However, when Offred finally takes her greatest risk and attempts escape, she exercises personal choice as an act of rebellion against the power structure. Thus, real power in any situation comes down to personal choice, and Offred's choice is her risky attempt to escape the system and survive.

Themes in the frame

Reconstruction and the creative process

The word "reconstruction" turns up several times in this novel, as a way of describing the creative process. When we use memories to create a story, we are not reproducing the past as it really was, but reconstructing it in light of all our experiences since the original incidents. Memories are thus fallible, and the past as reconstructed becomes a distortion that best serves us in the present.

Reconstruction works on three levels in *The Handmaid's Tale:*

(1) Offred's story is her own reconstruction, her attempt to select and arrange incidents, characters and details to describe and explain experiences during a period of about six months. She admits to manipulating her memories. She creates her "self" as she becomes more aware, discovering for us her hopes, fears and faults.

(2) The frame represented by the "Historical Notes" at the end of the novel adds another point of view, the historical "memories" of Professor Pieixoto trying to establish the facts behind the story Offred

has preserved on tape cassettes. In reconstructing what actually happened in the early history of Gilead, the scholar gives us additional details that Offred could not know.

(3) Margaret Atwood is herself invisible as creator of the world of Gilead. As our literary guide, the author does not prepare a separate students' or readers' handbook for Coles Notes. Instead, her fictional character, Professor Pieixoto, is our classroom instructor, providing background information on social and political elements of the novel, while keeping our attention focused on Offred. At the same time, Atwood's satirical approach, condemning the horrors of totalitarian rule, is clear. She also also adds her usual ironic point of view through her flawed, first-person narrators – Offred and Pieixoto – to make her reconstruction realistic.

Thus, in these three levels of reconstruction, Atwood demonstrates the creative process in operation. She leads us to an understanding of how her central character becomes a fully realized human being, with hopes, fears and faults that we can identify with. The fictional worlds of 1995 and 2195, seem very real and convincing.

Chapter Eleven

Utopia/dystopia

Margaret Atwood's novel *The Handmaid's Tale* is one in a long line of stories that depict supposedly ideal societies gone wrong. By creating fictional "anti-utopian" (or "dystopian") governments, writers criticize contemporary political and social situations and warn about developing threats to democratic freedoms. Usually the tone is satirical, though not humorous, as the writer exaggerates current public tendencies to ridicule abuses by those who hold power.

The word **utopia** was coined by Sir Thomas More in 1516, as the title of his fictional work of political and social criticism. More's *Utopia* satirizes the problems of sixteenth-century England, while depicting an ideal society on a far-off island. The word "utopia" is a pun on Greek words, *ou-topia*, meaning "no place," and *eu-topia*, meaning "good place," and now is used to refer to any society, real or fictional, in which some ideal form of government and universal happiness are the norm. In the oldest traditions of western literature – literature as old as the story of Eden in the biblical book of *Genesis*, or in the Greek philosopher Plato's *Republic* – two utopian ideas are embodied: a nostalgia for a Golden Age of ideal existence in the past and faith in the perfectibility of mankind and the creation of an ideal world in the future. Since More's time, many writers have tried creating their own utopias.

Near the end of the nineteenth century, historical events such as civil wars, revolutions, anarchist movements and worldwide conflicts undermined the belief in mankind's perfectibility. In the twentieth century, totalitarian governments became a reality. **Totalitarian** refers to a form of government run as a centralized dictatorship. Citizens are completely subservient in all matters to the higher ruling powers, on pain of prosecution and punishment. Hitler's Germany and Stalin's Russia are two examples among many.

Modelling their creations on the real world, writers began to use the concept of utopia in a new way. They imagined societies in which totalitarian rulers established themselves in power, usually through political or military revolutions, and progress toward the social ideal was halted in the cause of social stability. The ideal of individual happiness was defined by the authority of the totalitarian rulers. These "anti-utopian" stories constitute a sub-genre in utopian fiction; now the word **dystopia** (from Greek *dys-topia*, "bad place") is given to a fictional anti-utopian society, or "negative utopia."

A dystopia usually pictures a society in which restrictions dominate over individual freedoms, and the masses are closely controlled by a single dictator or small group at the top of an oppressive ruling class. Usually, no matter how distant the predicted future may be, the writer intends the image of totalitarian suppression of individual rights and freedoms as a satire on present conditions. Every dystopian fiction is meant as a warning of a potentially terrifying future that may arrive unless changes in present day social and political institutions occur.

An early example, the Russian writer Yevgeni Zamyatin's We, appeared (although not in Russia) in 1924. In English, the two best known dystopias are Aldous Huxley's *Brave New World* (1932), and George Orwell's *1984* (1949). The American writer Ray Bradbury published a less complex, but equally effective, dystopian novel, *Fahrenheit 451*, in 1953.

In *The Handmaid's Tale*, Margaret Atwood creates a dystopia in the Republic of Gilead. Her fictional society is an **oligarchy**, a form of government that is pyramidic in structure, with power held by a small group of rulers at the top. The Republic of Gilead is both a **military oligarchy** and a **theocracy**. The latter term refers to the right-wing religious elements in the structure, by which the rulers claim to act in accordance with God's will. In fact, Gilead is a monotheocracy (from Greek words *mono*, meaning "one," and *theos* meaning "god"), in which only the state-approved religion is permitted.

The chart that follows suggests literary elements that *The Handmaid's Tale* shares with Huxley's *Brave New World*, Orwell's *1984* and Bradbury's *Fahrenheit 451*.

Fictional dystopias

Title & Author (Pub. Date)	Setting	Main Characters
Brave New World Aldous Huxley (1932)	London, England, and Malpais (Savage Reservation, southwest U.S.A.) A.F. 632 (i.e., A.D. 2540)	Bernard Marx Lenina Crowne Helmholtz Watson John ("Mr. Savage")
1984 George Orwell (1949)	London, Airstrip 9, Oceania (England) A.D. 1984	Winston Smith Julia O'Brien
Fahrenheit 451 Ray Bradbury (1953)	unspecified city c. A.D. 2450	Guy Montag Captain Beatty Mildred Montag Clarisse McClellan
The Handmaid's Tale Margaret Atwood (1985)	Republic of Gilead (northeast U.S.A., area around former Harvard University: Cambridge / Boston, Massachusetts) c. A.D. 1988 Frame story: University of Denay, Nunavit, A.D. 2195	Offred Commander (Fred) Serena Joy Ofglen Nick

	Social Structure	Form of Rebellion	Conclusion
Brave New World	World State: rigid caste system; complete control of individuals by artificial reproduction and "predestination" techniques, sleep-teaching, social conditioning, and recreational drug (soma)	Bernard and Helmholtz: attempt independent thinking and behavior; make personal attempts to thwart conditioning John: suppresses love for Lenina; rejects World State civilization	Bernard and Helmholtz: exiled to island colony of independent thinkers with few civilized amenities John: condemns and punishes Lenina, then commits suicide
1984	Oligarchy: figurehead, "Big Brother," rules through Inner Party; control of daily life via two-way telescreens, thought police, constant rewriting of official history, economy and especially language	Winston and Julia: attempt independent thinking and behavior; make forbidden love in secret location; attempt to join underground rebel group, "The Brother-hood"	Winston: tortured and brainwashed in the "Ministry of Love," betrays Julia and is condemned to living death as an "unperson"
Fahrenheit 451	Centralized state control (details are vague) operating through Fire Department, destroys books, thereby suppressing independent or destabilizing thought by individuals; robotic aid: the Mechanical Hound, identifies and demobilizes criminals	Montag: hoards books; attempts independent thinking and self-awareness; contacts underground rebel group; escapes pursuit by forces of ruling authority	Montag: escapes with rebel group of hopeful book-memorizers, to safe distance from destroyed city
The Handmaid's Tale	Military oligarchy and theocracy; pyramid structure with power-elite at top; religion-based society; limited individual freedom; clearly defined and regulated role for Handmaids capable of bearing children	Offred: develops independent thinking, behavior and self-awareness; begins forbidden love affair; attempts escape with help of underground resistance group known as "Mayday"; later tapes audio diary of her time in Gilead	Ending unclear: Offred's diary breaks off, but frame story (Nunavit, A.D. 2195) suggests successful escape for her and eventual downfall of Gilead

Chapter Twelve

Atwood's style

From the beginning of her writing career, Margaret Atwood has been a successful poet, and throughout *The Handmaid's Tale*, she displays her poetic talents. A brief look at six areas of interest will illustrate the poetic features of her writing style and her use of literary techniques.

Diction

The first chapter illustrates Atwood's particular sensitivity to the rhythms of language and the connotations of words and phrases. Sensory appeals abound as Offred, lying on her army cot at the Red Center, in what was once a high-school gymnasium, imagines the sights, sounds and smells of long-gone games and dances:

> I thought I could smell, faintly like an afterimage, the pungent scent of sweat, shot through with the sweet taint of chewing gum and perfume from the watching girls, felt-skirted as I knew from pictures, later in miniskirts, then pants, then in one earring, spiky green-streaked hair . . . . the music lingered, a palimpsest of unheard sound, style upon style, an undercurrent of drums, a forlorn wail, garlands made of tissue-paper flowers, cardboard devils, a revolving ball of mirrors, powdering the dancers with a snow of light. (p. 3)

Note how the author piles on the sensory details, while at the same time suggesting the narrator's nostalgic feelings for the high-school activities that are now just memories, fading like the lingering sweat-smell that evoked them. Later in the same brief, introductory chapter, the poetic rhythms (and suggestions of rhyme) create an even stronger impression of Offred's emotional response, until the contrasting harsh reality of the present intrudes:

We yearned for the future. How did we learn it, that talent for insatiability? It was in the air; and it was still in the air, an afterthought, as we tried to sleep, in the army cots that had been set up in rows, with spaces between so we could not talk. . . . Aunt Sara and Aunt Elizabeth patrolled; they had electric cattle prods slung on thongs from their leather belts. (p. 4)

Imagery/figures of speech

Although Atwood's figurative language is usually subtle and unobtrusive, each metaphor and simile nevertheless conveys an emphatic emotional point, often in combination with other literary effects. For example, as Offred passes a round, convex mirror in the downstairs hallway in the Commander's house, on her way to the kitchen, she glimpses her reflection: "like a distorted shadow, a parody of something, some fairy-tale figure in a red cloak . . . . A Sister, dipped in blood" (p. 9). Her usual dress, like a religious sister's, a nun's, but blood-red, suggests the constant state of fear and danger in which she lives and associations with the female menstrual cycle and childbirth. Thus simile ("distorted shadow"), allusion (to Red Riding-Hood's danger) and connotation ("blood") interact to convey Offred's state of mind.

Another example of an effective simile that suggests Offred's state of mind occurs in a flashback episode. Describing the attempted escape through the woods, Offred drops an effective and appropriate image into a breathless, staccato-rhythm description of her panicked flight with her daughter: "There's breath, and the knocking of my heart, like pounding, at the door of a house at night, where you thought you would be safe" (p. 93). Here simile and speech rhythm together convey her emotional state.

Occasionally, a more developed image stands out as an analogy, a more complex statement of Offred's state of mind or her situation. For example, after her first illicit meeting with Nick in Serena Joy's sitting-room, she describes her reaction of fear and longing:

I lie in bed, still trembling. You can wet the rim of a glass and run your finger around the rim and it will make a sound. This is what I feel like: this sound of glass. I feel like the word shatter. (p. 127)

Later, on a shopping excursion with Ofglen, Offred uses another stand-alone image to comment sarcastically on the strictly limited freedom they have to walk in the city. She is probably remembering studies in an experimental psychology text she read at university:

Now and again we vary the route; there's nothing against it, as long as we stay within the barriers. A rat in a maze is free to go anywhere, as long as it stays inside the maze. (p. 206)

Allusions

It is entirely appropriate that a depiction of the Christian fundamentalist theocracy that is the Republic of Gilead should be full of biblical allusions. The basic idea behind the Handmaid system is itself drawn from the Old Testament passage quoted as an epigraph and read by the Commander as part of the mating Ceremony in Chapter 15.

Several characters, Aunt Lydia in particular, often draw on the Bible for aphoristic support, although Offred frequently adds her own bitterly humorous and sarcastic comment. For example, she recalls Aunt Lydia's injunction to the Handmaids to learn to "cultivate poverty of spirit. Blessed are the meek," an allusion to the Gospel of St. Matthew. Offred cynically adds, "She didn't go on to say anything about inheriting the earth" (p. 81). Similarly, at the Prayvaganza in Chapter 34, the Commander who conducts the multiple-wedding ceremony reads St. Paul's instructions about the proper duty of women: women are inherently sinful but "shall be saved by childbearing, if they continue in faith and charity and holiness with sobriety." This time it is Ofglen who adds the sarcastic comment, "He should tell that to the Wives, when they're into the sherry" (p. 277).

Literary allusions are also common in the novel, appropriate to a university-educated woman like Offred (and reflecting Atwood's own background, literary interests and fondness for wordplay). A good example is the line from John Milton's poem, "On His Blindness": "They also serve who only stand and wait." Milton's poem develops to this climactic thought, that they serve God best who, while suffering burdens imposed by God nevertheless stand prepared and waiting to be useful. The line is first used by Aunt Lydia, instructing the women at the Red Center in their roles as Handmaids (p. 23). Offred repeats the line as she waits in her room in the Commander's household and adds the thought from Samuel Beckett's play, *Waiting for Godot*, ". . . nothing to be done" (p. 64). Offred's room is, more often than not, her "waiting room" between times of limited activity such as meals, shopping excursions, and the monthly mating Ceremony. She may be waiting, prepared to be useful as a properly trained Handmaid, but she establishes also her impatience, her deep longings.

Symbolism

Symbols in Atwood's novel are often used in complex, interconnected ways. For example, a cluster of symbols associated with Serena Joy suggest the bitterness and sense of failure that Offred sees in the Commander's Wife. The possibly useless Angel scarves that Serena Joy knits have patterns of "stiff humanoid figures, boy and girl, boy and girl," like scarves for children (p. 15). They symbolize Serena Joy's failure (so far) as a mother and her longing for a child of her own – "her form of procreation," says Offred (p. 191). The knitted figures also symbolize the regulated, conformist society in which Serena Joy lives out her bitter role as a Wife in the social hierarchy. Her arthritic leg, requiring the use of a cane, suggests the crippled state of her present life, after an earlier career as a televangelist and controversial advocate for the duties and responsibilities of stay-at-home wives and mothers. Her garden, despite its beauty and promise of new growth and life to Offred's senses, is for Serena Joy a scene of mutilation, "snipping off the seedpods . . . . aiming, positioning the blades of the shears, then cutting with a convulsive jerk of the hands." Offred describes the Wife's actions as "some blitzkrieg, some kamikaze, committed on the swelling genitalia of the flowers" (p. 189); instead of harvesting the seeds, Serena Joy is destroying the flowers' potential for propagating new life.

Assigning symbolic meanings to settings, objects or people is most effective when the symbols enhance our understanding of theme or character. Another example will demonstrate how efficiently and forcefully Atwood links symbols to theme and character. The games of Scrabble, illicitly played by Offred and the Commander in the privacy of his study, are at first a surprising and, to Offred, somewhat absurd twist on the Commander's character and the relationship between them. But when we consider Offred's (and

Atwood's) fondness for wordplay, and the society's strict rules against reading, we can understand the symbolism attached to the Scrabble games. Building half-forgotten language from individual letters, drawing on past experience for ideas, enjoying the "feel" of exotic words and even the sensuous physical sensations of the smooth Scrabble tiles, giggling like school children over attempts at cheating by inventing words – everything about the Scrabble games Offred and the Commander share symbolizes the freedoms Offred would most appreciate in her daily life. Instead, the games end and she must return to the restrictive, controlled life of conformity outside the Commander's study.

Irony

An author's use of irony is always an unspoken compliment to his or her readers. We are expected to understand the unstated significance, for example, of characters' names, or specific incidents. Often we learn to appreciate the author's unexpected "twists" or reverses played on the implications in specific episodes. In *The Handmaid's Tale,* there are many instances where Margaret Atwood seems to wink and say, "Here's what I wrote, but you and I both know what this really means."

Consider the "Aunts" – Aunt Lydia, Aunt Elizabeth and the rest. Their title is ironic, since in real life an Aunt is often a doting and indulgent protector of nieces and nephews. In Gilead, the Aunts carry electric cattle prods and use torture to punish and control incorrigibles like Moira. The name of the Republic of Gilead is also ironic, an allusion to an Old Testament region noted for its fertile fields. The proverbial "balm of Gilead" was a medicinal ointment made from tree resin and metaphorically may refer to any soothing influences in life. Gilead in Offred's time is far from a healing or soothing society. For a third example, look at the name of Commander Fred's Wife: Serena Joy. As Offred points out, the dominant female in the household is neither "serene" nor "joyful." She is crippled by arthritis and bitter in the limited domestic role that she herself once actively espoused in public appearances. Now she tends her garden, taking out her anger and resentment by attacking the seed pods. She carries out a kind of savage, "blitzkrieg" mutilation of the flowers (p. 189).

Atwood's major ironic twist lies in the "Historical Notes" at the end. A symposium of academic researchers enjoy the scholarly pursuit of historical clues and long dead victims of the Gileadean dystopia. Pieixoto, the keynote speaker, even indulges in suggestive, male chauvinist jokes at Offred's expense. Such scholarly activities are cold, unconcerned about the real dangers and cruelties depicted in Offred's account. Meanwhile, we have experienced – through Offred's own words – the nightmare reality. We have followed the Handmaid's day-to-day struggle to make sense of her present situation, her past losses and her possible salvation in the future.

In all these examples – and many more could be added – Atwood's ironic "subtext" keeps us constantly aware of the reality beneath Gilead's appearance of organized stability. At a personal level, danger, cruelty and fear are the forces that make up Offred's nightmare existence.

Style and structure

In the novel's opening paragraph, Atwood uses the word "palimpsest" to express Offred's nostalgic awareness of the past (see above, p. 130). This unusual word is an important clue to Atwood's stylistic method and to an effective technique for structuring her story.

A palimpsest is a manuscript or parchment that has new text or drawing inscribed as an "overlay" on older writing that has not been completely erased. An "afterimage," faint traces of the original, show through the overlay. "Palimpsest" is a metaphor for Offred's whole story. We are always aware of the contrast between the traces of the past constantly on the narrator's mind and the harsh reality of the present. Whenever Offred pauses in her story to comment on her situation, or to meditate (frequently in the interlude chapters called "Night" but elsewhere as well), she provides glimpses of the past. These include her own past, the immediate past history of the country that has become the Republic of Gilead and the cultural past of western civilization. These traces show through, emphasizing the cruelties of the present and developing more fully Offred's character. As in a palimpsest, the past has not been completely erased.

Color symbolism in the Republic of Gilead

The levels of the social hierarchy – the classes and their specific functions in the pyramid structure of society – are marked by the colors of their uniforms and ordinary clothing.

- **Black:** *Commanders* – Black is commonly associated with dignity, power and influence but may also suggest the iron hand of autocratic rule, as in the "black shirts" of fascist Italy in the 1930s.
- **Blue:** *Commanders' Wives* – Blue is the color of strength and purity. In Christian art, blue is associated with the Virgin Mary. It is ironic that the powerful Wives, incapable of being mothers themselves, should be symbolically related to the Christian doctrine of the Virgin Birth.
- **White:** *Daughters in the Commanders' families* – White suggests angelic youth, innocence, virginity.
- **Red:** *Handmaids* – Offred herself implies that red, the color of blood, represents birth and new life, appropriate for the Handmaids' function.
- **Khaki:** *Aunts* – Khaki, dull brownish-yellow, is always associated with the military. The Aunts, with their strict discipline enforced by the use of cattle prods, are like army instructors, drill sergeants.
- **Green:** *Military (Angels and Guardians); Household servants (Marthas)* – Dark shades of green are military colors, the uniform of those who serve higher authorities.
- **Striped (red/blue/green):** *Econowives* – Appropriately, the Econowives, multi-functional wives of men low in the hierarchy of power, wear mixed colors.
- **Gray:** *Unwomen and others in the Colonies* – Gray suggests lifelessness, even the grave. Those sent to the Colonies are dead to society, especially since their duties involve cleaning up hazardous waste.

Chapter Thirteen

Essay and seminar topics

1. Atwood's frequent use of wordplay in the novel reflects her love of language. Defend and support this statement with specific reference to Offred's playfulness with words, features of Gileadean society, and biblical or other allusions.

2. Identify Atwood's references to feminist issues of the 1970s and 1980s. Create a chronology of events and prepare a commentary that traces the evolution of these issues.

3. Explain how each of the following symbols is linked to a major theme of the novel:
   (a) cattle prod
   (b) red Handmaid's habit
   (c) missing chandelier hook
   (d) *Nolite te bastardes carborundorum*
   (e) Scrabble game
   (f) the Wall
   (g) the rope at the Salvaging ceremony
   (h) gaudy costumes at Jezebel's

4. In discussing *The Handmaid's Tale*, Atwood said, "I wanted my book to be firmly based on human nature and fact. There's nothing in it that we as a species have not done, aren't doing now or don't have the technological capability to do." Select and explain a variety of practices in the Republic of Gilead that are extensions of historical or contemporary occurrences.

5. In the novel, a small elite group of religious fundamentalists deny basic human rights to the masses. Identify, rank and document the most serious violations of human rights in Gileadean society. Justify your choices and ranking.

6. Identify the totalitarian measures used in the Republic of Gilead to retain centralized power and control. Provide specific examples of each totalitarian measure.

7. Human beings are capable not only of resisting oppression, but also of retaining personal integrity and responding courageously in the face of unspeakable suffering. To what degree are these three qualities demonstrated by Moira, Offred and Janine?

8. Read another dystopian novel, such as *Brave New World*, *1984* or *Fahrenheit 451*. Compare your choice with *The Handmaid's Tale* as a satire, with specific reference to contemporary issues: population control, forced participation in government-controlled activities, limitations on personal freedom, recreational activities.

9. Writers of speculative fiction often create futuristic societies whose strengths and weaknesses have immediate relevance to our own time. Explain and illustrate how *The Handmaid's Tale* provides commentary and warnings about our contemporary world.

10. Harold Pinter's screenplay for the film version of *The Handmaid's Tale* made significant changes to plot and characters of the original novel. Explain at least three such changes in detail, and suggest reasons for those changes.

Chapter Fourteen

Theme model essay

Assignment: *Identify an important theme in Margaret Atwood's* The Handmaid's Tale, *and explain how it is developed and illustrated. Use appropriate references to characters and incidents in the novel as supporting evidence.*

Surviving Gilead

In Margaret Atwood's *The Handmaid's Tale*, three forms of power are evident in the structure of Gileadean society: institutional authority in the Commanders' political and military control; domestic authority in the Wives' control over "women's business"; and individual influence through covert resistance and rejection of authority. Analysis of the hierarchical social structure reveals the truth that personal choice on an individual level constitutes real power, despite institutional restrictions and domestic controls imposed from above.

Institutional authority in Gileadis male-dominated, residing in the Commanders, although their specific political, military and religious functions are never clearly

---

Commentary

Introduction
(a) cites title of work and author
(b) breaks down three levels of power to be examined
(c) states controlling idea or "truth" – i.e., important theme

First subtopic
(a) defines and illustrates highest level of power: institutional controls
(b) notes additional privileges associated with high-level authority

---

defined. We never see Commander Fred actually on the job, whatever his job is, although there are many examples of male dominance throughout society. For example, Commanders preside at religious functions, such as mating Ceremonies and Prayvaganzas. They also enjoy certain privileges, limousines with personal chauffeurs and private clubs like Jezebel's, where they mingle with foreign businessmen or indulge in illicit sexual activities. Finally, if Professor Pieixoto is correct, Commander Fred (Frederick R. Waterford) was directly involved in the early Sons of Jacob meetings, planning the coup that established the Republic of Gilead and its patriarchal authority. Below the Commanders in the power structure are the elite fighting forces, the Angels, and then the Guardians who guard city barriers or serve as sentries and personal assistants in the Commanders' households. Outside the structure are the secret police, who control individual lives through torture and intimidation. All these power roles are filled by men.

Domestic authority resides in the Wives who control "women's business," everything to do with the role of the Handmaids in the household and in the procreation of children. Serena Joy, for example, early in the novel sets the limits for her new Handmaid, Offred, determining when she should stand or sit and which door she is to use. She also warns Offred at their first meeting about limitations regarding her relations with the Commander. But Serena

(c) demonstrates with specific references that institutional power throughout social structure is male-dominated

Second subtopic
(a) defines domestic authority as "women's business," focusing on Wives' areas of control in social hierarchy
(b) focuses on Wives' important symbolic part, and real control, in Handmaid system

Joy exerts her dominance in more important ways. In the crucial mating Ceremony, the Wife has an important symbolic role, but she also exerts real physical control over her Handmaid during the sexual act. In the event of a successful pregnancy, she would – like Commander Warren's Wife – take part (again symbolically) in the Birthing ceremony and assert her claim to any healthy child produced by the Handmaid. Eventually, she would give away that child in an arranged, group wedding, like the one demonstrated in the Prayvaganza of Chapter 34. Below the Wives in the hierarchy are the Econowives and then the Marthas. Outside the structure are the Aunts, responsible for the training and control of Handmaids. Men may have ultimate authority over the social structure, but the underlying domestic authority is built on the influence and control held by women.

The third form of power is at a more personal level, through individual influence operating covertly, outside the institutional and domestic hierarchy. At this level, Offred gradually learns to exert her own limited power. For example, the Commander's willingness to break rules gives her a bargaining tool and allows her some choice. She learns to see the human side of the man who had previously been only a symbol of oppressive authority, and she chooses to forgive him. That too, as she says, is power (p. 168): forgive an enemy and you change your relationship putting yourself to some extent in control. Similarly, her relationship

(c) emphasizes female-dominated authority underlying the whole social structure

Third subtopic
(a) uses numeric link to breakdown given in introduction ("third form of power")
(b) focuses on Offred's growing awareness of the power she holds at this level of personal choice
(c) illustrates two central relationships: Offred and Commander Fred, Offred and Serena Joy

with Serena Joy changes, when the Wife indicates her willingness to circumvent the rules and arrange a liaison between Offred and Nick. Offred can choose to cooperate, thereby exercising some power in this situation. Her understanding of this bitter woman whom she hates gives Offred another basis for personal choice and limited control. Other female characters also demonstrate how personal choice in resisting authority undercuts the Gileadean power structure. For example, Moira chooses to serve as a prostitute at Jezebel's, rather than face death as an Unwoman in the Colonies. She illustrates how individual choice may exploit the system's weaknesses. Ofglen's personal choice moves her to the extreme form of resistance, when she takes her own life rather than be tortured into betrayal of the Mayday group. These women strike at the heart of the Gileadean system, and from such examples, Offred is moved to make her final choice, to take her greatest risk, and attempt escape. She too exercises personal choice as an act of rebellion against the political and domestic power structures that have for too long controlled her life.

Ultimately, then, real power, no matter how oppressive and restrictive the political authority and domestic controls may be, comes down to personal choice: to covertly withstand authority and risk one's life on the chance of escape and survival. Offred has learned to trust her own choices, and despite institutional and domestic control by forces of oppression, she will survive.

(d) compares other female characters who exercise choice: Moira and Ofglen

(e) demonstrates that Offred's final choice expresses her rejection of, and dominance over, institutional and domestic authority

Conclusion
(a) restates controlling idea from introduction
(b) clincher: reaffirms Offred's real power in choosing to survive

Chapter Fifteen

Model seminar

Assignment: *Prepare a seminar presentation on the purpose of Offred's story-telling in Margaret Atwood's* The Handmaid's Tale. *Focus on the connection between memory and the preservation of sanity and self.*

Story-Telling and the Preservation of "Self"

Introduction

    1. Definitions: (a) Story-telling means reconstruction of the past from memories.

                       (b) Reconstruction means not reproducing the past, but re-interpreting past experiences in light of events since.

    2. Controlling idea: (a) Memories are unreliable; the past as retold is a distortion that serves the story-teller's present purpose.

                       (b) As story-teller, Offred's purpose is to preserve her sanity and maintain the integrity of her "self."

Subtopic A: Reconstructing Her Past

    1. In Offred's reconstruction, she selects and arranges incidents, characters and details to explain her life in Commander Fred's household (Ch. 7, p. 50).

2. Offred admits that reconstructions from her memories
   may be false:
   (a) example: escape attempt in the woods and fate of Luke
       (Ch. 18, p. 128);
   (b) example: first sexual contact with Nick
       (Ch. 40, p. 327).
3. Offred creates her "tale" to recreate her own character after
   temporarily losing her "self" in the traumatic "lost time"
   following the loss of her daughter (Ch. 7, p. 49).
   She gradually fills in details of her past life, her role in the
   present social structure, her hopes and fears, and the
   choices available to her (Ch. 23, p. 168; Ch. 24, p. 179).

Subtopic B: Preserving Her Sanity

1. After traumatic "lost time" following escape attempt, Offred,
   drugged and possibly electro-shocked (Ch. 7, p. 49), relies
   on story-telling to rebuild her sanity and sense of control
   (Ch. 7, p. 50).
2. Offred almost despairs after bad dreams of the past but
   "hoards" sanity as a valuable possession, saving it to "have
   enough when the time comes" (Ch. 19, p. 135).
3. Offred clings to FAITH in the past (note symbolic cushion) and
   HOPE for the future by telling her story to future listeners:
   "I tell, therefore you are" (Ch. 41, p. 334).

Subtopic C: Maintaining Her Integrity

1. Central to Offred's story are her self-deprecating humor, her
   self-critical honesty:
           (a) example: "washed, brushed, fed, like a prize pig"
               (Ch. 13, p. 85);
           (b) example: "buttered . . . like a piece of toast"
               (Ch. 17, p. 120);
           (c) example: participation at Red Center in mocking
               Janine (Ch. 13, p. 89);
           (d) example: shame re memories of Luke and affair
               with Nick (Ch. 41, p. 334).

2. Offred maintains the integrity or wholeness of her "self":
    (a) example: Janine, loses her "self" to system
        (Chs. 13, 22, 33, 43);
    (b) example: Moira, maintains integrity of her "self" by
        choosing life at Jezebel's; exploits system's
        weaknesses to her own benefit (Chs. 15, 22, 38–39);
    (c) example: Ofglen, chooses self-sacrifice by suicide to
        protect others in Mayday resistance group
        (Ch. 44, p. 356; Ch. 45, p. 357);
3. Offred chooses to risk her life; hopes for escape and survival
   are centred on her trust in Nick (Ch. 46, p. 368).

Conclusion

1. In telling her story honestly, Offred discovers for us her fears, her faults, her hopes.
2. She thus creates her own character and maintains the integrity of her "self."
3. The institutional and domestic pressures are trying to disintegrate her identity, her sense of self. However, instead of becoming one interchangeable part in the social system, Offred survives as an individual.

Chapter Sixteen

Annotated bibliography

Atwood, Margaret. "Author's Note on *The Handmaid's Tale*," and "An Interview with Margaret Atwood on Her Novel." *The Handmaid's Tale*. Toronto: Seal Books, 1986, 1998.
Informative insights by the author about the sources of her novel and its implications for contemporary society.

Davidson, Cathy N. "A Feminist *1984*." *Ms.* February 1986: 24-26.
A very positive appraisal of the novel, including several sharp insights by Margaret Atwood herself.

Ehrenreich, Barbara. "Feminism's Phantoms." *New Republic* 194 (17 Mar. 1986): 33-35.
Critical of how "thinly textured" this dystopia is; raises background questions regarding structure and operation of the society. Emphasizes the complicity of feminist and anti-feminist forces in the creation of a "feminist dystopia."

French, William. "Pessimistic Future." *The Globe and Mail* 5 Oct. 1985: D18. A generally positive review of the novel, but French points out – as several other critics do – that Atwood's cautionary tale perhaps takes on too many subjects.

Gray, Paul. "Repressions of a New Day." *Time* 10 Feb. 1986: 84.
A positive review, emphasizing the "beguiling" and "fascinating" qualities of Atwood's novel, while criticizing the lack of "chilling plausibility."

Larson, Janet L. "Margaret Atwood's Testaments: Resisting the Gilead Within." *The Christian Century* (20 May 1987): 496-498. A detailed examination of many biblical references in the novel, to build a complex religious interpretation of Atwood's feminist stance.

Malak, Amin. "Margaret Atwood's The Handmaid's Tale and the Dystopian Tradition." *Canadian Literature* 112 (Spring 1987): 9-16. Includes a useful, detailed analysis of characteristics of dystopian fiction, as applied to, and extended by, Atwood's novel.

McCarthy, Mary. "Breeders, Wives and Unwomen." *New York Times Book Review* 91 (9 Feb. 1986): 1, 35. Generally negative review from a well-known feminist author. McCarthy praises several features of Atwood's writing, but finds the novel lacks clear focus or direction as a cautionary tale.

Prescott, Peter S. "No Balm in This Gilead." *Newsweek* 17 Feb. 1986: 70. A positive review, with emphasis on Atwood's strengths as a novelist: her themes, her foresight, her use of irony, and her protagonist's individuality.

Sage, Lorna. "Projections from a Messy Present." *Times Literary Supplement* 21 Mar. 1986: 307. An uncommitted review: positive regarding Atwood's creation of Offred and her nostalgia for the "messy present"; negative regarding several loose ends in plot and message.

Stein, Karen F. "Margaret Atwood's *The Handmaid's Tale*: Scheherazade in Dystopia." *University of Toronto Quarterly 61* (Winter 1991/2): 269-279. Excellent analysis of the feminist point of view regarding the creation of "self" through language and storytelling.

Stimpson, Catharine R. "Atwood Woman." *The Nation* 31 May 1986: 764-767. Gilead dissected from a political point of view. Analysis of Atwood's satire on power politics versus feminism, includes clever comparison of several female protagonists in Atwood's other novels.

Timson, Judith. "Atwood's Triumph." *Maclean's* 3 Oct. 1988: 56-61. Biographical information about Atwood at the time of her seventh novel, *Cat's Eye* (1988), and comment on how much of the author can be found in her various female protagonists.

Updike, John. "Expeditions to Gilead and Seegard." *New Yorker* 12 May 1986: 118-126. A positive analysis of Atwood's novel: as a Canadian perspective on American culture and as allegory on the status of women in the mid-1980s.

Wilson, David A. *The History of the Future*. Toronto: McArthur and Company, 2000. A history of prophecy and prophetic literature, with several chapters on twentieth-century dystopian fiction, including *The Handmaid's Tale*.

Online Resources

Margaret Atwood: http://www.web.net/owtoad
Extensive bibliographies of works by and about Margaret Atwood, plus biographical information and links to The Margaret Atwood Society. An invaluable research source for students. Updated regularly.

Publisher: http://www.randomhouse.com/boldtype/
Research source for materials by and about Margaret Atwood. Includes interview excerpts with the author and audio links – Atwood speaking about her recent novels.

Film

The Handmaid's Tale Virgin/Cinecom/Bioskop Film, 1990. Color, 109 min.

Dir., Volker Schlondorf. Screenplay, Harold Pinter.
Photog., Igor Luther. Music, Ryuichi Sakamoto.
Perf., Natasha Richardson, Robert Duvall, Faye Dunaway, Aidan Quinn, Elizabeth McGovern, Victoria Tennant.
Beautifully photographed but marred by major changes to plot and character emphasis. Offred's simplified character is stronger, less sympathetic.
"Interesting, but best described as sterile." (Leonard Maltin)

Opera

The Handmaid's Tale by Paul Ruders, with Danish libretto.
First performed at Royal Danish Opera, Copenhagen, March 2000.
Radio broadcast: *Saturday Afternoon at the Opera* (CBC Radio 2), June 30, 2001.

Chapter Seventeen

Selected criticism

The following excerpts capture the essence of various critical reviews and analyses that appeared at the time of publication of The Handmaid's Tale. *You might choose one of these as a starting point for a thesis to be developed in an essay or seminar presentation.*

The story moves by flashback, meditation, and present-tense narration as the narrator pieces together what she remembers of her past life and knows of her present situation. Through her storytelling, she grows more politically aware and self-conscious. She resists the reduction of Gilead (her "reduced circumstances") by small acts of self-assertion, by fantasies of becoming strikingly visible (she imagines stripping in front of the guards at the barriers) and by the act of narrating her tale and thereby constructing a self.

Karen F. Stein, "Margaret Atwood's *The Handmaid's Tale*: Scheherazade in Dystopia," *University of Toronto Quarterly*

. . . But could it happen here? Some of it "is happening now," [Atwood] says. She is careful to distinguish her novel set in the future from futuristic fantasy. "It's not science fiction. There are no spaceships, no Martians, nothing like that." In fact, "there is nothing in *The Handmaid's Tale*, with the exception maybe of one scene, that has not happened at some point in history. I was quite careful about that. I didn't invent a lot. I transposed to a different time and place, but the motifs are all historical motifs."

Cathy N. Davidson, "A Feminist '1984'. Margaret Atwood Talks About Her Exciting New Novel," *Ms*.

[Atwood's] reach exceeds her grasp, and in the end we're not clear what we're being warned against. Is it the danger of a fanatical religious group taking control of the United States and imposing a tyranny similar to that in Iran? Or the possibility of our poisoning the atmosphere with chemical and nuclear pollutants to the point at which a normal birth is a rarity, and infertility threatens the survival of the race? Or the danger of the feminist cause over-reaching itself, resulting in a repressive male backlash?

Atwood's novel is in fact a cautionary tale about all these things. Any one of them would have been subject enough for a novel; but in her scenario, they interact in an implausible way to bring about the grim totalitarian world of tomorrow.

William French, "Pessimistic Future, The Handmaid's Tale by Margaret Atwood," *The Globe & Mail*

Surely the essential element of a cautionary tale is recognition. Surprised recognition, even, enough to administer a shock. We are warned, by seeing our present selves in a distorting mirror, of what we may be turning into if current trends are allowed to continue. A fresh post-feminist approach to future shock, you might say. Yet the book just does not tell me what there is in our present mores that I ought to watch out for unless I want the United States of America to become a slave state something like the Republic of Gilead whose outlines are here sketched out.

Mary McCarthy. "Breeders, Wives and Unwomen," *New York Times Book Review*

. . . Atwood means to do more than scare us about the obvious consequences of a Falwellian coup d'etat. There is a subtler argument at work in *The Handmaid's Tale*, and it is as intellectually interesting as the fictional world she has housed it in. We are being warned, in this tale, not only about the theocratic ambitions of the religious right, but about a repressive tendency in feminism itself. Only on the surface is Gilead a fortress of patriarchy, Old Testament style. It is also, in a thoroughly sinister and distorted way, the utopia of cultural feminism. . . .

Barbara Ehrenreich, "The Handmaid's Tale," *The New Republic*